Published by:

Wherever Books LLC
A Division of Renegade Company LLC
Littleton, CO 80127
www.whereverbooks.com

Roku Channel:
Wherever Books

MW01247994

Angel

ANGEL

BY T. ULICK

Trigger Warning

If you are sensitive to obscene language, graphic descriptions of explicit sex acts, use of language describing bodies that is not anatomical and is degrading, dirty dialogue between despicable and disgusting characters, please do not read any further. This book will upset you and you will be offended.

If you are suffering from any form of physical, mental, verbal, or sexual abuse, or suffer PTSD from such abuse or other types of violence or harm, please, shut this book. It will trigger you throughout.

If you have religious beliefs based on the teachings in the Bible, either one or both Testaments, this book contains concepts and references to religion, clergy, and Christian teachings that will upset and offend you. This is not a book about the *Bible* or of religious teachings and creates its own narrative of God, Angels, and demons. It will upset you and offend you. It is suggested you stop reading now.

Terry Ulick
Author

أنني كنت أكتب هذا الكتاب بدلا من ذلك. كنت أحد نسخًا من
البرامج والويب طوال اليوم، وأعود إلى كتاب السلوك في مكان
العمل. لكن الكلمات كانت هنا، وليست الكلمات التي اعتقدت
أنني كتبتها. عندما انتهيت، جلست لتحسينه ككتاب للطباعة، وأثناء
تجميع الصفحات، نظرت إلى الشاشة وكان هناك هذا الكتاب

توقفت، واندهاش من الملف الذي وضعته في برنامج معالج النصوص
أكان السلوك الصحيح. لم يكن الكتاب الذي اعتقدت أنني كتبته،
وبالطبع كنت مع خبرا من أمري وفي حالة من عدم التصديق

بعد أن تجاوزت المفاجأة، بدأت في قراءة ما كان على الشاشة، وهذا
صفحات هذا الكتاب الذي تملكه الآن. كان مثل أي شيء، قرأه من
قبل، ولا شيء، بمكنني كتابته. وجدت نفسي أشعر بأن كل عاطفة
ممكنة للبشرية كانت جميلة ومضحكة وحزينة ومرعبة وملهمة
وبهيجة أكثر من كل ذلك. أعلم أنها كانت حقيقة. كل ما قيل هنا
حدث. إنها قصة الخلق، الحياة، الجحيم، الخطيئة، الشر، الخير،
الفرح، والملائكة. كما أنه يحتوي على الشخص الذي يطلق عليه

From the Scribe

I would like to take credit for authoring this amazing story, but I had no part in that. I was merely the scribe used to capture the words that follow using a personal computer.

Sitting down to write a book about workplace conduct, I wasn't aware that I was typing this book instead. I would take a break or stop for the day, return to the workplace conduct book but the words were those here, not the ones I thought I was writing. When finished, I went to format it as a book for printing, and while formatting pages, I looked at the screen and there was this book.

Stopping, wondering what file I had placed into the page makeup software, it was the right file. It wasn't the book I thought I had written, and of course I was confused and in a state of disbelief.

Getting past the surprise, I began reading what was on the screen, filling the pages of this book you now hold. It was like nothing I had ever read, and nothing I could have written. I found myself feeling every emotion possible for the story was beautiful, funny, sad, horrific, inspiring, and moving. More than all that, it was truth. All told here happened. It is the story of Creation, Heaven, hell, sin, evil, good, Joy, and Angels. It also has the one we call satan, although that it is just a scribble written in some desert by someone afraid to say the true name of the fallen one.

Reading where all things came from, why we suffer, I read the story as that — but also as a story of two young women seeking love and independence from their family ties. It is the coming-of-age story of an Angel, and one who isn't an Angel. There are moments of love like I had never read anywhere, and sacrifice that is beyond anything ever told. It is not just the story of Creation, it is the story of all of us. We all go through a time when we become individuals and follow our own path, not the ones our parents planned for us.

Researching if any other books or authors had experiences where some entity used them to tell a story they weren't aware of when they were writing, I discovered that it has happened before. There are authors who sit with a pen, eyes closed, and their hand begins writing in a language they didn't know, or about something they had no knowledge of. I can only accept that I was the scribe who copied down the words given to me from some Angelic or Divine entity.

Thank you. It's a great story and I get to put my name on it!

I hope there is a sequel. I want to know what happens next.

Terry Ulick
2023

Angel

Preface

Know that although I, Gloria, have been in existence since the time First Angels were made, I am not a First Angel. I am the True Angel. Born of the First Angel, Michael, and the Second Angel, Ethereal, they were created and never born or grew from infants to young adults then grownups. I was the first Angel born, a special honor.

I am not yet fully a woman, if that, for I am still young and foolish. I speak true that all, even the Creator, say I am the Holiest and most beautiful of all Angels. I know that I am beautiful as all Angels are such, but I think only that all treat me kind as I have suffered more than can be understood. Though the first born true as Angel I was also the first to know shame, loss, and be an object of desire only because I am beautiful. All beauty comes from within. My form is fully my spirit and soul and I can not be any less than the beauty I am, and that has been my curse.

The Third Angel was Lucifer. He is my uncle. He is insane. He exists only to have me, but that shall never be. What he has done to have me since I was a sweet child of six playing in the fields of Heaven is beyond Knowing.

To have his sick pleasure, me, Gloria, he devised the fall of Angels where they would live in what you know as hell. That was never for freedom or independence. He wished to have his own domain where he could act out his perversions without anyone stopping him. The fall was intended to include my mother, Ethereal, his sister, thinking she would never leave Heaven without me, Gloria. Being the most Holy of the First Angels, she was aware he planned to harm me, so fell from Grace, leaving me with my Father, Michael, with Lucifer thinking she had me by my hand in the mad rush to fall.

Once the fallen landed in the horrendous place Angels call abaddon, learning he could never return to Heaven and that I was not there, he grew so enraged that he transformed

into the hasataan, the satan, the dark lord of rage. From
him grew the serpent, a thing none should ever know or
see, and the serpent impaled my mother, leaving me
alone with my father, Michael.

I grew not as a child, but as daughter of the one who built
the Arch to defend Heaven from any of hell. I was the
daughter of the ArchAngel, Michael, and I took the
mantle of ArchAngel to help him find a new love.
Though still a young woman, I am the mightiest
Angel of all, the true ArchAngel, the Guardian,
the Avenging Angel. Doom to any not holy.

This is the story all must know. How a young girl,
sweet, loving, kind and innocent, is also the most
feared warrior in all of existence.

I, Gloria, am the Guardian. I am the line between
good and bad.

If you follow hasataan, the satan, my uncle, Lucifer,
it is time to begin praying you never meet me, for
you will be no more.

Gloria

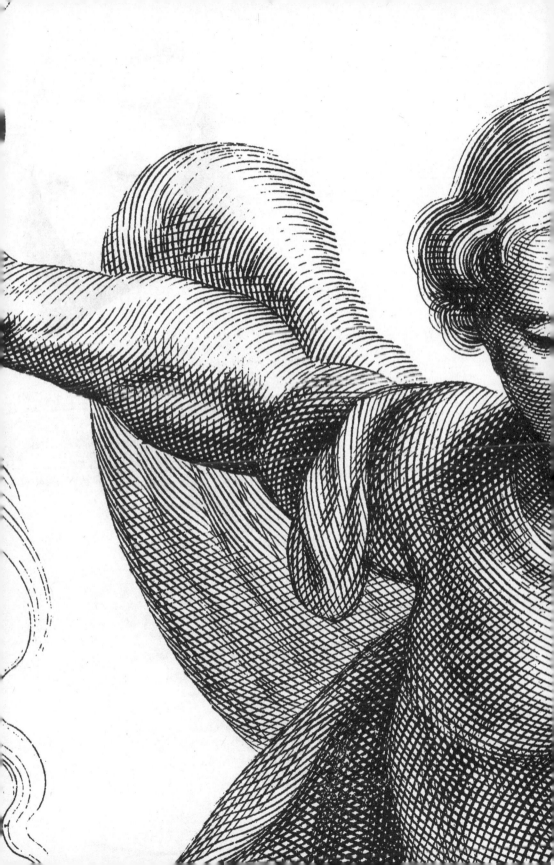

Scroll One

What has always been is no more.

Sitting on what any who traveled such distance would deem
the edge of all creation, Gloria sought no solace or isolation.
From afar, the glorious one could see billions of lights ones not
Knowing called stars. Knowing there was no end to such lights
above, below and on all sides, she was far beyond thoughts of
whatever infinity is, or called. Such thoughts belonged to ones
never having a card game of chance with the Thought she called
Father, just as her father called the Thought his Father. Her
eyes smiling, she was the wayward child who confronted the
Thought, saying the deck was stacked and the Father was skilled
at slight of mind. Tired of such dogged dogma, feeling taken, a
rube, she took Wing and created a gust that sent playing cards
flying, revealing they all had the same number. Ten. Later, telling
Michael, her father, of her ire, he was impressed, revealing he
had only reached sevens in the game. The Thought that made all
things had high opinion of her, he proclaimed.

"Father. If you are proclamating, please, rise off the ground with
your right hand up in the Knowing way. How can I know you
speak true if not?"

Looking at him with complete sincerity, they each smiled,
then laughed, then Michael took a deck of cards from a basket
and threw it in the air proclaiming he was as wayward as his
daughter, but perhaps not as brave.

Such was a fond memory, and a fond memory was comfort
facing all creation. All around were the twinkles made long ago,
many with places where creatures roamed, played, cried, suffered,
and sought a deck that was fair.

It had never been fair. Or, as the Thought had philosophized,
perfectly fair.

Thinking most often the hand dealt to most held only twos, it was the most difficult game for any to play. Two states of being. Alive, or nothing. Happy, or sad. Hurt, or joyous. Respected, or despised. Important, or ignored. After a thousand years of listing the opposition pairs in a deck of twos, she came to the one that held the most trouble for her.

Good, or bad.

For another thousand years she thought of bad and how it destroyed good. It was truly the most rigged deck of any. Speaking to no one and nothing, she closed her eyes in pain.

"Good has a line. Rules. Bad? It has no line. It is without end."

Not banished, not denied, she left the place she called home to think of all decks played, knowing she would eventually think of the deck of twos. A full deck with 52 cards; every card a two. A choice of good or bad. Knowing that one such as her had no choice at all, she could only choose good. Yet the Thought held the cards close to the vest, saying that all were Graced with Free Will, and all had a choice. Even her, the Supreme Guardian, the one who wielded the Blade that could send the bad, the evil, the ones choosing to harm the good to nothingness.

"No. I can only strike if I am struck. Attack if attacked. Defend, never prevent. Where is a choice in that? What is Free Will if I can not decide?"

Her Wings rose up in straight lines, one leg rose up slightly, her Blade blazed in front of her lighting her form and revealing a Majesty none other in existence had. Looking upward, she ascended without stopping, going faster than the light of the fires called stars, faster than a thing of matter could go for she was not made of such stuff. She too was a thought, an idea, a wish, a hope, a thing beyond knowing to all but her father, her uncle, and the Thought. No longer able to include her mother, she was a thought no longer, cast to nothingness by her uncle, the one who must know her Blade. The one who had a choice, made it, and chose to do wrong, never right, with such gift.

Rising endlessly, there came a moment when she wished to understand what falling was to those who fell. With that wish each feather of her Wings flew away from her. They were light and they left her in the darkness of the nothingness where none had ever dared go. Wings gone, she leaned back to stop her ascension, put her arms out to each side, her head back fully, her long blonde hair floating for a moment as she went from rising to a full fall. Seeing the dark of infinity above her, she saw her hair rise to straight lines above her from falling down, not caring, not thinking, not Knowing. She left all that was thought — feeling only the fall and nothing more.

Beyond time that could be counted, she continued to fall, thinking only once.

"Without thought, nothing matters."

In time, how long she cared not, lights once again appeared, surrounding her, now only streaks in her Vision, blurs, and nothing more. Then just as quickly the light ceased and darkness returned. Crossing to the nether side where none had ever ventured, she thought once more.

"My uncle made a choice. To be here where none go."

Thinking of the Fall, the eventful day she lost her mother, she knew soon she would be where those who fell with her uncle had landed, followed by her father to rescue them. Now, the nether place would know his daughter. It was a fall through all existence, taking infinity to hit the place called rock bottom in rumors and legends. The Thought had given it a name.

Abaddon.

It was her uncle's domain, the one he chose to fall to while taking others Angels with him, telling them they had a new home. A lie. Her uncle was the deceiver. He fell only to have her when she was but a child. A young girl trusting all those she knew, including her uncle. He created the hell, the pit, the abaddon, all that is horrible — only to have her. His lust. His craving. His sickness. His perversion. His insanity. All bad was created by him to have her; to satisfy his sickness. He impaled her mother, his sister, because she fell without taking her with. It was on that day, hitting rock bottom, denied his craving for a child that he transformed into hasataan. His desire for her, never ceased, but on this day she would fall and hit rock bottom.

With that thought, she crashed into blackness hard and cold. She landed in her uncle's home.

Touching the rocks, her Wings appeared once more, blazing in blinding light, a Blade in her hand. Crouching, ready to strike, eyes blazing blue beams of Divinity should any evil come near, looking at the depraved souls surrounding her, all cowering with fear, she spoke.

"Uncle. The Sweetness is here."

Her voice, not a sound, a trumpeting torture to the minds of the fallen ones, the minions, the lost, the depraved, the ones who never fell but sinned to join the hasataan, caused screams of agony in the endless cavern that held no comfort except suffering, the light from her eyes, her Wings, blinding them, making them blinder than they had ever been for they could only see the dark of evil, not the blaze of Glory she offered. Like she thought them lost, they thought the same of her. Rock bottom was their forever home and she did not belong there. Hearing mutters of despair, she cast the blue rays of pure light from her eyes to any who made such sounds, striking them down in terror, sinews once hands covering the orbs that were once eyes. Slowly, they backed away forming a large circle around her, backs to her, hoping she would never look their way. Seeing them was not the reason she was there. She paid them no attention as she shouted once more.

"Uncle. I have something you must have."

Up from the black granite in front of her, a shape rose and took form, the form changing from black rock to the form of the evil that was once beautiful, once Graced, once cherished, now still beautiful but hideous. She saw him as spirit, not just form. His once-white sheath was now black as the cavern. He stood in a shadow even in the blaze of her light. Knowing he was both Lucifer and the demon hasataan, he sought not to repel her or battle, but to act as he had once before the fall. Gentle, calm, hands open in welcome, a soft smile on his face. Under the form she saw his true nature and it was not smiling, and not beautiful. It revealed lust for her, his tongue licking as if deep inside her sacred places, his eyes locked on the space between her legs as she stayed crouched, legs apart, covered only in gossamer. His tortured skin was sweating from seeing what it craved for so long. His whole form under his guise was shivering in lustful spasms. She saw the serpent appear, looking at her, forked tongue out making licking motions, eyes locking on hers as it began growing. It existed for one reason. Her. To enter her, take her being, and consume her Grace to give majesty to Lucifer. He was the dark that craved her light. A wanderer who saw her as his home. Looking at her, not hiding his need to enter her, feasting on her entire form, deep into each part, his eyes rolling over her curves then down into her shadows and mysteries. No other being was beautiful in his Vision, only her. He had given all he was to have her — and had been denied.

"Sweetness you are. We both know what Joy you offer and that only I deserve it. Gloria, I have given all I was to be in Union with you. Do you not understand what I have sacrificed to give you my Joy?"

Watching his serpent grow, it was past being controlled for it had a mind of its own, yet existing only to serve its master. It was the vile creature that entered her mother the time of the fall, rising up through her taking her heart's Joy, her hope, and her faith. Taking her very being it stuck its slithery head out of her mouth, licking her juices from its face as Lucifer, as hasataan, sent the serpent slithering in the air, displaying Ethereal, her mother, as its conquest for all to see and to learn the power of the serpent. It was the first act of such evil any in all creation had ever known, and the moment that changed good to bad, Joy to sorrow. He took the soul of Ethereal for no reason other than to strike ire in Gloria; to have her come to the darkness to avenge her mother's fate and there in the abaddon be feasted on.

"No, uncle. Your mind is corrupt. You take Joy, never give it. You took my Joy for you took my mother, your sister, the one who loved you. I see your serpent. Know this, uncle. If it hisses once more, if it does not shrink back into your soulless form, I will use my Blade to cast it for your minions to feast on. My Blade is true. I am here to strike. I will start with that sick thing you made."

Making no sound, the serpent recoiled and as if never there, gone.

"Sweetness, it meant you no harm. I exist only for you. I know you want the serpent. To take it in you and be master of it. You are the only one it will not consume. It is to pleasure you, nothing more."

Without a word, Gloria rose, letting her Wings float above her forming a circle of light shining on her alone. Still holding the Blade, her gossamer faded away, leaving her naked and showing her perfect form and beauty. She floated in air, naked, the most beautiful in Creation as her beauty came from within. Her form and being were identical. She circled once for Lucifer to see all of her, then faced him, staring into his eyes now smoking and showing flames inside his pupils.

"This, uncle, is what you shall never have."

In the next instant, she was clad in crystal armor, even more erotic to Lucifer. She was a sight to behold like he had never known before.

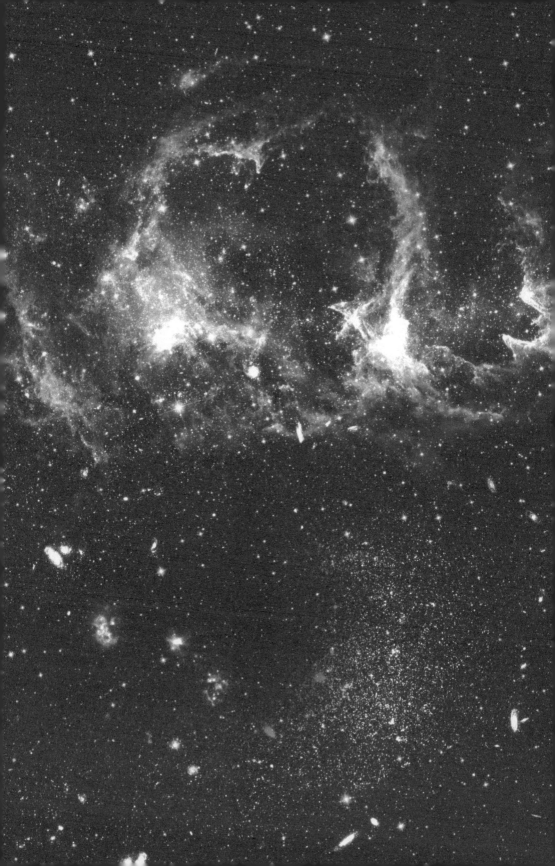

Scroll Two

Putting the bowls and plates just washed after eating their dinner on the sideboard, Gloria recalled how her mother had made them, watching her spin a pottery wheel and make them out of clay in the dirt around the hovel her father had made before she was born. Wiping the cooking pot dry and putting it on a shelf, her father asked her if she'd like to go outside by the small pond where they could lay with their feet in the cool water and gaze at the stars in the clear night sky.

Excited at the idea, Gloria gathered some cherries in a basket she had made from reeds, again thinking of how her mother had taught her to weave and make things from nothing. Walking to the pond, Michael held her hand and her other swung the basket gently as they found their favorite place to lay and stargaze. Like all nights where they lived, the weather was nicely cool, a gentle breeze blew, and the sky was free from clouds. Laying down, she felt overwhelmed by the glistening lights above them. There were more than she thought possible to ever count, though she knew she could count quite well. There were so many stars in the sky that it looked silver, blue, purple and many other colors. It was a tapestry like she had seen one time in the cabin where Father, the Creator, lived. Marveling at the large cloth of thread making the tapestry, she asked Him who made it.

"Ethereal did. Your mother was so sweet, and I was so gifted knowing she made it for Me. I will treasure it forever."

It was the first time she had ever heard the word, "forever." The Creator thought her to be quite smart, so she somehow failed to mention she didn't know the meaning of the word. Looking at the stars she saw a patch of black in them, and that made her think of what it was.

"Father, look! There's a hole in the tapestry above… See, there… That black part. How come there's a hole?"

Michael followed to where her finger pointed, and turned to look at her expression of surprise and wonder. He smiled knowing she was yet to learn what the black area meant, and how curious she was to know as much as she could about all things. Thinking of how to explain the sky above, he knew she would want a full explanation. He had long abandoned simple parables or make-believe stories for the mysteries of existence for her. She was too smart and knew when he was taking a shortcut. After a visit to the Creator's cabin not long ago, she was bold in telling him she thought the Creator was crafty with His answers and had called Him on His explaining how birds learned to fly.

"Father, He sat on the porch eating apricots and told me they just somehow knew how. I told him just because I'm a little Gloria doesn't mean I'm falling for that story. He got even more flustered when I asked how come they have Wings and we don't. He didn't have an answer for that, either. Then, He almost swallowed a pit when I told Him that He was supposed to know everything!"

All he could do is be amazed at the gift she was to both Ethereal and him. She was wondrous. Wishing Ethereal could have been there to hear such a story, sadness was quick to wash over him as she was up in the place where the black was. In the endless nothingness of eternity. He was there the time her existence ended and it was a trauma that would never go away. He missed her. Each time he looked at Gloria he saw Ethereal for Gloria was so like her in every way. Smart, perceptive, affectionate and loving. They looked so much alike. Each had beauty shared between them that no others had. Much more than their long blonde hair, perfect features and beauty, they radiated Joy and offered so much kindness he was ever in awe of them. Ethereal lived on in Gloria and in his heart and thoughts. That couldn't change that he wished to hold her hand, look into her eyes, hear her breathing next to him at night, or the sound of her voice. All that was gone. She was in nothingness now.

Still pointing to the hole in the stars, Gloria waited for an answer. Michael knew it was time to explain the nature of existence to her. Having asked him many times where her mother had gone, it would help her understand that like all in the Father's Creation, they all came from nothing, and there would come a time when they may return to nothingness just as Ethereal had. Gloria had told the Creator, the Father, she needed real answers, and Michael wished only to tell her the real story.

"That's not a hole. That's just a place where there are no stars. All the color and twinkles are stars floating in that blackness. They go on and on, forever it seems. There are so many that from here we see them like a tapestry above us. One behind another, on and on. It's beautiful, do you agree?"

Sitting up, looking at him, she agreed it was but asked what was behind the last of the stars they could see. He could only smile as she asked the most perfect questions. That was the most important question anyone could think of when studying the night sky.

"Well, that's a wonderful question. I asked Father that same question before you were born and, well, you know how He answers things. He said this and that, and had all kinds of opinions. I don't know... I think you and I are too alike. In the middle of all His talk, I grew bored and thought of an even better question. I asked Him where did He come from."

Eyes wide, a look of surprise, Gloria gasped.

"You asked Him that? Really? Oh, father, you are my hero! What did He do? Did He try to shut you up with some fresh apricots?"

Laughing, they both shook their heads for the Father had done such things to each of them when the questions became tricky. They were alike, and both enjoyed the way they could get the Father in a tight spot for answers.

"No, He surprised me. You know all those scrolls He has in that cabinet I built for him? He went and rummaged through it and took one long scroll out and just gave it to me."

Gloria's face showing shock, she asked what happened after that.

"He offered me some apricots!"

Growing hysterical, they both knew Father didn't want to be accused of beating around the bush, or being asked where the bush came from. Looking back up to the night sky, Michael said that the apricots had been most delicious, but even better Father had given him the scroll to keep, saying he would have use for it one day. Gloria said she had wondered what the scroll up on the high shelf was all about, and asked if that was the one.

"Yes, I treasure it. I doubt there is another one like it, or even if He has a copy although He could always Create another if He wanted. He is very crafty, I agree. He knew one day there would be a little Gloria and you would ask such a question. Oh, I'm certain He gave me the scroll to read to you so He wouldn't have to face you standing there with your hands on your hips waiting for an answer."

Nodding, she smiled knowing exactly what he meant, telling him she was sure that was the reason. He laughed with her, then started to get up.

"I'm going to get a new candle, bring it here and you can light it. I'll bring the scroll with and use its light to read it. Just look up to the black up there as I read, or close your eyes if you wish. This is the perfect time of day to learn about the black space up there."

Getting up, he went to get them and also brought back a pitcher of water and cups. Placing the candle between them, Gloria held up her first finger and a small flame appeared above it as she moved it to the wick of the new candle made of wax bees had made for them. Untying the string around the scroll, it rolled open and it was filled with glyphs and looked quite long. Taking a deep breath, Michael began reading the story of how all things began, and what was there before they were there. Gloria listened, fascinated at how wordy the Father was even in a scroll. He read it from the beginning, and stopped at the end. The scroll began with a word neither knew.

Genesis
How I Made All Things, Even Me

Thinking was being, yet not being enough. Once, there was nothing. Taking what some call time, it had been nothingness for all eternity, yet there was no meaning to eternity. With nothing, nothing matters. Within the nothing was the Thought. It didn't know it was alone or what it was. There was nothing to compare itself to. There was no beginning, and if there was, that too mattered not. Nothing mattered, there was nothing but an awareness of being. Existing. Nothingness was what existence was, and there was no way to know anything other.

Yet in nothing was the Thought. The Thought existed and had eternity to do what a Thought can do. Think. Yet, think about what? The answer was there was nothing to think about.

Unexpectedly, and for no reason that could be understood, the Thought had a consciousness that there was nothing, and nothing to think about. At that moment, there was something. A realization, a Knowing, an understanding, a concept, something more than nothing. The Thought had made something that had never been before.

An idea.

At the instance of the idea, it was so powerful that the idea sent a ripple in the nothingness. The ripple had never been, and in the nothingness was the idea radiating outward to forever.

Then the Thought had another idea. The idea was more than nothing, and it wasn't a thought, it was different as it had come from the Thought, and then after the idea came a realization that the idea could not exist if it had not been created by the Thought.

Where nothing had happened forever, something changed for nothingness no longer existed. The Thought had made a thing. Some thing. It was something new and at that moment the Thought realized it could make ideas, realizing if there were many ideas put together, it would be something in the nothingness. Instantly ideas began erupting, and something was happening. Each idea was rippling outward, and they began merging and when they joined together they were no longer just ideas, they became something more than the Thought had considered. Something more than thought, something apart and not needing the Thought any longer. They became things.

All the Thought could do is think, and for a long time it thought only of how the idea became something new. At one point, the Thought considered that things created were created by thinking, and it could be where, with enough thinking, any thing could be made. That thought caused a ripple that sent all things thought of into places far away from the Thought, and that was something never thought of. The nothingness must be a thing as well.

That sent the Thought into a quandary as It had only known Itself, and had no idea that nothingness had a form, an existence, that it was where it existed. Thinking long of what nothingness was, an idea formed that it was a thing. A big thing where ideas could exist and have a place of their own.

Such an idea created a flow of thoughts of pure fancy and whimsy. Ideas about something that was not like nothing. With that one idea, a thing was made. It was a clump of something being imagined that took form. It existed and was not an idea. It didn't think, it did nothing, it just was there, suspended in the nothingness. The Thought knew it was there, for it was the idea to be just that. Something in the nothingness that was not a thought. The next idea was how could that be known? It wasn't that it didn't exist, but in nothingness, it could not be appreciated for the great idea it was.

Then the idea formed that if the Thought could perceive it somehow, envision it as more than a thought, that would be an even better idea. The idea of envisioning it in thinking was lingering. Knowing of it, there was a wish to have true Vision of it, not just the thought of it being there. A ripple stronger than any other was coming from the Thought, and in that ripple was the idea taking form. All about the Thought, nothingness, for the first time, could be seen in Its mind. There, all around, was nothing, and it was nothing to see with Vision, but nearby was the idea that was just a clump of something that had taken form, and was there, yet black as the nothingness. It could not be seen with Vision, and the darkness of nothingness was upsetting to think of. In time the idea came that the thing sitting there should be different than the darkness of nothing, and at that instant, the thing became light. It was just a thing, but it was light, not dark.

Then, the Thought considered that the light may just be a thought, an idea, and nothing more. Yet, what if there were another thing close to it, not light. A clump of something thought of. Would the light let it be seen? That was an idea that struck excitement and it could reveal if it was real. In that instant, another clump formed near the one that was light. It amazed the Thought, for the one made with light let the one without light be seen. Suddenly, thoughts of things to surround the light began and all around the light were little clumps, all just things, yet all more than seen, they clung to the light, and wanted to be near it and be seen.

That was delightful. The Thought realized the light made things like it be seen, and the thought of delightful was how it felt to see such things, once made, exist on their own, doing what such things wanted to do. The Thought hadn't made them to cling to the light, it was their own idea. They had ideas and they were made by ideas, but not like the idea once made. This was unexpected, and for another eternity the Thought kept making more things, and they began to take new forms and some were fire, some not. Throughout the nothingness were things lit, things clinging to them, each light heading out to the places where they were the only light, and in Vision, nothingness had been changed into something incredible. Into the vast endless dark were lights and shapes and in the darkness that had been the only thing known, there was light all around, and they had their own will, going where they wished, the little blobs following them, circling around them, and the Thought was in the middle of something amazing to behold. It had all been made from one idea, and the Thought had created all things.

Just existing, the Thought began to consider that the things all around had form, yet the Thought did not. It was all marvelous to think about, to have Vision of, yet there was a thought, a deep one, lurking, that it should be more than the Thought. It wanted to be something that could be seen, and have form, could touch the things created.

Forever a mystery, the Thought wished to be something. And it happened. There, in the nothingness, the Thought took form. It hadn't considered what form It wished to be, for It had no idea of what It should be. But somewhere in thoughts were ideas It wasn't aware of, for how else could a form never thought of exist, or come to be? The Thought realized It hadn't thought of blazing light or round globes circling them, so those were mysteries as well. The Thought accepted that thinking was a thing itself, and it had a form of Its own and It must have created it as there was once nothing else. That was good. The power of creation was not something to think about. It was something to let happen.

In the places where there were no globes or lights, the Thought had become something fully different from all that had been created. Realizing It had sight, not only Vision, but the Thought could also see what It had become. It was unthinkable, marvelous, and for the first time ever a sound was heard, had voice, and ears, and could have thoughts take form as something ears could know. Words, the thoughts became things, and the Thought used the voice to shout out to all It had made.

"Meet your Maker!"

Scroll Three

Long since the Thought had created all things, wanting to have other thoughts and not be alone, the nothingness had been made into a place where the Thought, having form, could feel things beautiful and learn what else could be created. Like making Its own form, a place took shape, and It was not like the rest of all created. It was a place the form could have to think of what would come next. It started as a place to walk and thinking it would be nice to have things to touch, things began to appear. Giving them names, they were grasses, trees, rivers, clouds, hills, mountains. On and on it went, and the place was more than anything envisioned, and like the first light, the things made began doing things on their own. One day, walking to a pleasant grove of trees, there were new things hanging on them. Red, round, and all different from each other in some way. Ones hung from the trees, some had fallen off and were on the ground. Not thinking why, the Thought bent, took one from the ground and bit into it. There was no reason to do it, but it happened. Again, a ripple shook all things in all places. The thing, like nothing known before, was wonderful to bite, then without reason once more, swallow. Feeling it inside, it felt good, and more biting, then more of them from the branches.

That was a wonder, and the Thought started to roam and look at all created there, and found more things to bite, and in the rivers was water to drink. Never thinking of why, there was too much to stop and think about. Using voice, they had none. They were not thinkers, they were things that thought existing was enough, and wished nothing more. They were happy to exist. But the Thought felt something happening inside the form. A longing to have more than the things around them. Another thing that was also Thought. With voice, with a form like it had, a thing to share all the wonders with and hear each other.

With eyes, they closed. Thinking of one to talk to, one to share creation with, when opening the eyes, both Vision and sight saw a form walking and it said, "Hello."

The thing had thoughts, and was like in form, but different. The Thought wanted one similar, but not one who could create all things. It just made sense, there could be only One that started all things. The one walking came and sat, looking all around, and said all created was beautiful, then said the most unexpected thing.

"I am Michael. I am of You and from You. I am but a child, and I thank you for I would not be without you."

The Thought was overwhelmed with Joy. Looking at Michael, words came that were never planned.

"Michael, I am your Father. This is your place. Your home."

Smiling, something that made the Thought feel delighted once again, Michael asked if there were any other Children, for it would be nice to all be together. Thinking, again, without knowing why as it had never been thought of, the answer was clear. Make another, and make one like the trees where they could bear fruit of their own. Long watching how fruit came to be, how flowers bloomed and spores flew to make new flowers, out from the woods where Michael had walked from came one like Michael, but a flower ready to bloom. Michael would plant seeds, the other would make more like them. Like the flowers, the second one was beautiful as Michael, but like the most beautiful flowers, had an attraction that was more than the form. A beauty beyond the form.

Walking to them, Michael held out his hand, and said to the new one, "I am Michael, and this is our Father."

Sitting with them, the new one looked into their eyes, touching them both, then said, "I'm Ethereal."

As they started talking, the Thought listened to them and was amazed that they had Knowing. Each knew what they were. He asked Ethereal if she knew what she was created to be. She smiled, then laughed.

"Of course! What a silly Father you are. You know what we are, You made us. Michael is a man, I am a woman, and we are your Children. We're like the nature around us, and we are from You, and we love You. But I love Michael too. In a different way, for he is not my Father, You are. I am sure we are meant to be with each other, and our love is to please You. But I don't know more than that, and I am not sure why I know that, but I do know it is true. Michael, do you think as I do?"

Watching them, Michael smiled at Ethereal, then put his arm around her and pulled her to him, and that had a power greater than the blazing lights in the sky. The Thought realized the creation of the two was the most wonderful thing to ever be. They had what was longed for. Love. And they loved Him.

Suddenly, inspired not feeling alone any longer, without even being aware of it, more Children started walking from the grove. It was wonderful, not planned, but made perfect sense. Many Children to fill the wonderful place. Ones to love their Father, and each other. None alone as Thoughts in nothingness.

The next child made walked to them and they greeted him, for like Michael, he was a man. As he sat, Michael introduced him to the Father, then each other, asking the new man his name.

"Lucifer."

They sat, all smiling, admiring each other, and they waited for a woman to come and join Lucifer. None came. Others walked hand-in-hand, Knowing what and who they were, waving at them. Lucifer stopped smiling, clearly feeling different, and alone. He asked his Father if one had been made for him, like Ethereal and Michael had been made to be together. Michael and Ethereal looked at their Father, and they too were worried and wondering where the one for Lucifer was. The Thought was mystified, and there was no answer as there had never been a thought of such a thing. Wishing to calm Lucifer, an answer came. A thought. An idea.

"Lucifer. All is new, and new to Me. I know that one will be for you and will be one most amazing. Not here yet, but one day, not long ahead, she will arrive, and you will know. Worry not, child. Creation is a mystery to you, to all, and Me as well. Have faith in your Father. Like an apple on the tree in the grove you walked from, one will come, and she will be sweet, yes, one who will be your sweetness."

All Lucifer could do is nod. He looked around, seeing all the others walking hand in hand, him sitting alone. He felt different. He asked a question as he had worry.

"For such a wait, when others do not, will she be the most wonderful of all?"

Nodding, the Father smiled, telling Lucifer that when she appeared, she would be glorious.

Scroll Four

Crouching, thinking only of driving the Blade through Lucifer, she watched him hold up his right hand, rise just above the hard stone, and speak true as he did when an Angel in the Father's home.

Between them was a Vision of the day he was made, sitting with her father and mother, and the Creator, the Father, being told one day his love would come and she would be the most beautiful of the Children and she would be glorious. The Vision faded, and he remained in air, hand held in Proclamation.

"You have never known this, have you?"

Gloria shook her head, not letting the Vision sway her. She told him he was a deceiver and the Vision was a lie as he had not shown he was already vile and insane, there was nothing to feel sympathy for. He had Free Will, he knew he was sick and could have asked for help. He remained, listening, looking at her, and he was thinking. He answered.

"Of course you think it a lie. I was once that, and now I am the deceiver. What else could I be? I was promised, by our Father, that you would come and would be with me. You came, but we were not one. You loved me as your uncle, not as my mated one. All around me were mated. I waited for you, and you are just as Father said. The most beautiful, and sweet. But Gloria, he said you would be my sweetness. Do you say Father does not speak true? You know that Vision is not a lie. I can not make that Vision. That is true. Ascend and ask the fool is that is what happened, and what was promised to me. And you wonder why I am what I am? You have all you were promised…"

With that, the entire cavern was white with blazing light. All cowered except Lucifer, who remained in stance before her. Gloria rose far above him, Wings filling the cavern just as it filled galaxies, her Blade held high above her head. She looked down at him, and in a near whisper, she answered.

"You dare say I have all I was promised?"

The entire cavern of abaddon began to shake and cracks were forming as the anger of Gloria shook the fabric of Lucifer's domain. The ones cowering began running from them, seeking a place where they would not be consumed by the chasms opening in the ground to swallow their sad souls. Staring only at Lucifer as her ire was destroying his world, she whispered again.

"You stole my promise."

In the space between them a Vision appeared. It was Ethereal, her mother, impaled on Lucifer's serpent, her existence being eaten by it while all his fallen ones watched and did nothing. Behind Lucifer, cowering, his minions cried out in pain and agony, all fearing the same fate, turning from the sight as it was too horrific to be seen by even the most vile demons there.

"My mother, Lucifer. The promises she made to me. The promises that I would be with her forever by the Father. The promise of a life together, to be like her, to love her. That promise was taken from me. By you. Do you dare deny it? Speak true. You know the Blade will do so if you do not."

The Vision fading, Gloria lowered to float directly in front of Lucifer, the Blade sideways over her left shoulder ready to cast him to Nothingness. It would take only one lie, one look, one threat, one sneer and the Blade would end her tormentor forever. Lucifer knew her only intent was to strike, and that could only be if he lied.

"I will never deny it. I ate your mother, and Gloria, sweet she was. Not as sweet as you will be. You were promised to me. If that Blade casts liars back to nothingness, then ascend, stand before Father, ask Him of His promise to me and why He lied. Let the Blade send Him back to where He came. He belongs in nothingness for creating all this. You think this is my doing? Father created all things, remember? He created evil, sin, abaddon... Me, Gloria. Me. I am His doing. His creation. He created your suffering. I did what He made me to do. Free Will? Are you free to strike me down right now? You want to, but you can't. And, you know why."

She did. If anything Lucifer said was a lie, the Blade would have struck. It hadn't. They both knew what that meant.

Rising just slightly above him, Gloria looked at him with disgust.

"As a First Angel, you are smart, and you play the rules to your liking. Know this, creature, I will return after I talk to Father. I will tell Him I too am smart, and I too will play the rules to my liking. I will have Him make this Blade do my bidding, not the bidding of rules long played your way. I will be free to strike because it is right to stop you forever."

Faster than can be understood, Gloria's Blade and Wings rose straight up, and she flew beyond matter, at the speed of her thought, leaving Lucifer standing, sure of himself, knowing he would have his Sweetness one day as the Father would never think He was wrong.

Lucifer stood, able to see what others in abaddon could not. He watched Gloria rise, her beauty impossible to not follow. Like her, his powers were that of a supreme Angel and he could travel at the speed of thought, his thought being to be close enough to her ascent that he could continue viewing her Heavenly form. With her crystal armor, she was more enticing than when naked. She had taken battle garb to torture him with the memory of the way she looked. Never cowering to him, always above him, he found pleasure in her dominant manner and ways. In all eternity, only her father, his brother, Michael, had no fear of him. It was certain that Gloria now had no fear of him. They held the Blade, the destroyer of all it struck, intended only for him. Blade in hand, they had no worry of his might. Never deceiving himself, he knew even without the Blade they could prevail in any battle with him. They were as him. First Angels with the strength of the Creator. A strength he once had, and surrendered when he went wayward and defied the Creator. He had power, but no majesty. If he had Gloria, he would have her majesty for she would surrender it to him. Since the fall, his only thought was how to bring her to her knees, before him, in full submission.

Trying all ways to have her understand all in creation would suffer if she didn't give herself to him, no unheard of act caused her to waiver in her disgust of him. After defiling the legion of First Angels falling with him from Grace, after creating hate, sin, perversion and all things unholy, after bringing sin to the new Children of Earth and corrupting them without mercy, Gloria never understood that all such terror would stop by her descending to kneel before him and take the serpent... as her mother had.

Never one to admit what he did was wrong, he had long realized impaling Ethereal, Gloria's mother, was a reaction, nothing more. It was his anger that Ethereal had fallen without bringing Gloria to abaddon with her that caused him to have ire so intense he became the monster, the hasataan, the demon with the serpent that impaled Ethereal as its first act of vengeance. He could control the serpent, but knew he could not control himself when it came to Gloria. He would do anything for her.

Following her through all eternity, he was close enough to see her from behind, and was so close he could touch her. Knowing she was aware he followed, she refused to turn or stop. She could easily stop and wield the Blade and strike him, and he had hoped she would at least pay him that much attention. He thought of calling out to her, saying he wished to surrender, to stop all evil, but being a lie, the Blade would strike him. It was what she hoped he would do, and it must be she who surrendered to him, not him to her.

In what was but a moment to Angels of their might, they were at the Arch, the entrance to Heaven where no demon may enter. She hadn't gone to Earth or any other place. She went to the one place where he would have no standing or way to deceive. All stopped, and they were standing facing each other. Gloria was under the Arch, Lucifer in front of it. She stood in striking pose, ready to strike if he moved towards her in any way.

"Enter, Uncle. Enter. I welcome you home."

Taunting him, he grew aroused, excited by her power over him. He wanted to kneel before her, have her look down at him, and let him taste what he had hungered for since she was born.

"My home will forever be you, Gloria. I am nothing without you. I am nothing now, in my sick pit of despair, but you could change that. Make all sin vanish. All will be like before the fall. Cast the Blade aside, walk to me, let me put my head where I can taste you, let my Angel love have what it was promised. My Sweetness. Stop all sin and suffering. Come to me."

Walking to the Arch from the fields of Heaven came Michael. He was in a simple linen sheath, his hair long and flowing in a wind that blew only for him. He was as beautiful as the first day made, but his face had a sadness for the loss of Ethereal, and for Lucifer for he was his brother. Gloria hadn't moved and showed no sign of hearing his plea. She remained in striking pose, the Blade was humming, its light blinding bright, making her blonde hair flow from its force making her look stunning, like he had never seen her before.

Walking up to her, Michael rubbed her shoulder, telling her that Lucifer had lost his way and he would talk to him.

Walking past Gloria and the Arch, Michael went up to Lucifer. He held no Blade, and had no worry. He had only looked at the ground where the line he drew in the sand there remained since made. It was the division between Heaven and hell. Lucifer began laughing at him.

"Oh, Michael. You still can't see the arrogance of all this. I can not cross that line, go past it, but you can. You can go to abaddon, just as your daughter has done to taunt me. Yet, I can't go home. I can't go to my farm, see my four horses, visit my niece, or you. Is that righteous? I think not. Have you ever given that any thought?"

In many ways it was as when they were both in Grace, brothers, before the fall. Having a talk, challenging each other with a philosophical question. There was no struggle, no battle, no ire. There was no Blade between them. Michael knew Lucifer would say or do anything, but none of it was for good reason. It was all only a way to get Gloria. He was not vengeful. He could talk, be polite, but he couldn't be fooled.

"Brother, why bother? You have fooled all in eternity, even many of the first Angels. You will never deceive me. You will never change Gloria's resolve to strike you to nothingness. Yet, here you are, as if anything you say means anything. A lie means nothing except to the liar. You are making a fool of yourself. What do you think this will accomplish?"

Feigning innocence, Lucifer could not stop himself from being the deceiver. The question was sensible, and Michael was right. He could only speak true, or the Blade would speak his doom.

"Do I think it will bring Gloria to me? No. Do I think she will strike? Yes. But brother, you will never understand this…"

Michael watched closely, and for the first time he saw a glimpse of truth in Lucifer's manner. A desperation. A hopelessness. He was more tortured than he had ever imagined, and it was something to be worried about. Lucifer knew he was revealing his torture, and saw no reason to argue it, at least not with the Blade so close.

"Yes. Both of you, look at me. Since made, since I stood before my Maker, I had a promise. One hope. That I would have a Sweetness, my own, just as you had Ethereal. And there she is. Right before me. What I was promised. What I have thought of without stop. What I was made to have Union with. I am a starving Angel and there, just in front of me is what will fill that hunger, but the branch is just higher than my reach. So, I starve. I suffer each day. You have no idea what that has done to me. You have seen my wrath. That is nothing. Nothing. What will come if this continues is not even a hint of the wrath that comes next. There will be new words when I cry out. Words that will change all that has ever been made. That will destroy all things. The Father was once only a Thought. He came from nothingness. There is a place that is less than nothing. It is an endless desert. All that is known will know that place, for it is my mind and I will swallow nothingness and all that followed. It will be mean nothing to me, but everything to all creation. I will have Gloria. With all things once I swallow all there is, or will ever be…"

Lucifer had Willed himself away. Michael and Gloria stood at the Arch, waiting, for he may return. Michael turned to her and shook his head.

"He wasn't lying. The Blade would have struck."

Scroll Five

"What is that one?"

Michael pointed to a flower he had never seen before. Unlike all the other plantings in the lush garden that had long been there to admire, all growing entwined together to form a visual feast, the new bud was in a patch of rich soil, a large square with no other plants near and having only one leafless branch with it for support.

More than a place of beauty to both eyes and vision, the multitude of flowers sang in a symphony that was theirs alone. Some who visited thought the music to be praising the One who planted them; created them from thinking them into being. Others believed it was apart from the flowers, something that emitted from the mind of the One who was once pure thought, now in form they called Father. The One knew what they believed the sound to be, Knowing that such wonder could be whatever they wished. It was not His to decide, such was the way of Free Will. The music was theirs to be what they needed it to be. Either way, all knew it was Joy, and a delight to hear.

Looking like the Angels in Heaven, the One, the Creator, the Father, the Thought, had no need to be different than the Angels. They all were made in the image of the Thought long ago. Never out to impress, what was inside the form of the Father was so powerful there was never a need to question that others were made and faced the Creator of all things. Michael, the first made, held no position or place of honor. Being the first meant nothing. Just a chance, a thing that happened as one had to be first. First or last, all were what they were; none higher or lower; none more favored. If Michael held any position of favor, it was only because he had been there longest and had suffered the loss of his love, Ethereal, the second made. Michael understood that existence was fleeting and fragile, even for an Eternal Angel. Existence could end, even for the Maker.

Bending to see the newest addition to the garden, Michael could smell the fragrance yet heard no song. The Father walked to where he was and crouched down with him, looking at the delicate bud.

"That, Michael, is your daughter."

Not yet in bloom, there was a single bud on a vine that was tall and needed the branch for support as it grew. So white it illuminated the plants around it, Michael knew it to be a rose, but roses had only been red until the new variety being in front of them. It was magnificent, pure, had no thorns and one day would blossom to a state of beauty that would be overwhelming. He nodded, looking at the bud, then the Father.

"I thought that may be, yet You told her long ago she was the red rose. When she reached for it, with other plants on each side, it had thorns that pricked her finger. You explained she was the most beautiful flower ever known, but that beauty made some want it enough to take it against her Will. The thorns were to protect her flower, and she learned that she was not safe with Lucifer wishing to take her. So, she is no longer the red rose? No need for thorns or protections, as this rose is beyond even the red but has no thorns. Has she seen it?"

"She will. There will be a time when she needs to know her place in My garden. Though she will be inspired by it, it will be for the one who loves her one day. A gift for him, and she will always remain a gift of a flower to the garden. For now, she remains the red rose. Thorns are needed. She will understand."

Looking, such news surprised Michael as he had no Knowing that any was destined for his daughter. He was moved for he worried that would never be. The Father understood his thoughts.

"That is something I wasn't aware of, but it is comforting to know. But I have a question. Why alone? Why not with the other flowers? With the red rose?"

Standing, the Father nodded, looking at Michael, then to all the other flowers surrounding them. Michael stood, looking at the garden, then back to the lone white bud. Looking at him, the Father smiled.

"You know well she is unto herself. She feels the way this flower makes you feel seeing it. Isolated and alone. That is but a feeling, not what is. She is right to feel that way. So, tell me what you feel when you see the white rose…"

Tears were forming in Michael's eyes, coming from his soul. Being filled with a sadness that only he could know, he let his tears fall, leaning over the bud, letting them grace them, glisten on the white curves, adding his feelings to the flower the same as he had given to Gloria since the day Ethereal was taken by the serpent.

"The same as the day of the fall, when she was little, here with you. Taking a branch to fight off her uncle, her pretend Blade. She has never let go of that branch, and it was to protect me. Her whole existence has been to avenge the taking of Ethereal. To never feel safe, and You know she isn't. She has no peace. Lucifer is relentless."

Father looked sad, and cried tears that drenched the soil of the new rose.

"This rose is alone and not with the others for the only moisture it grows with is my tears, Michael. It grows from the pain of loss. Each day I kneel here and cry. Each day the rose grows stronger from my sadness. And now, yours. If you wish, visit each day, and give it what is needed, with Me. I know her pain, and that is what creates My tears."

Filling with emotions matching the day his love, his wife, his Joy, impaled before him by his brother when abaddon was created, Michael could not restrain himself.

"I will. Know this, for I speak true. She is child with a branch no longer. She is the only Angel who leaves Heaven, and she wields the Blade, and you know she wishes only to strike him with it. It is where a change must come. Father, she has no fear of facing Lucifer, and before coming here I found her at the Arch, and Lucifer was there behind the line. She had went to abaddon to taunt him, make him follow so he could do anything where the Blade would strike. It is not that she will be harmed for the Blade will stop him if he does anything to threaten her. That is not my worry…"

Pointing to a bench fashioned from stone, the Father sat and waited for Michael to join him. Once seated, the Father reached down to the path in the garden and took a handful of soil, smelling it, then opening his hand.

"Her taunting your brother makes him like this soil. Look, as I grow tired of holding it I let it slip through my hand. Lucifer's mind is slipping, more than ever before. Her taunts are letting what soil remains fall completely away. It is not what Gloria will do that worries you. It is what Lucifer will do. Is that the concern?

"Yes. When at the Arch, I went to greet him and he spoke of how You broke Your promise to give him his mate and that it would be the sweetest one, and that can only be Gloria. He says you lie and have broken a promise. Then, he told Gloria all evil would stop, all would return to Glory if she was his. She told him that will never be. That is the worry. He said he has had enough, and he is ready to destroy all things, You included, if he doesn't have Gloria. He said as you were part of all things, it would be the end of you."

The soil that fell had formed into a small sculpture of Lucifer, and at Michaels last words a wind came and blew it away to where flowers grew.

"Michael, with or without Gloria, he wishes to do such. I have thought of it, and I will say that is his wish and why the Blade did not strike. He wants to, for only then can he think himself powerful as me. I created all, so he wishes to destroy all. It was no easy thing to create it, and will be harder to destroy it.

Scroll Six

"What do you want of me? I want nothing of you."

Under the black granite of abaddon's cathedral, the place that had no end any could reach, was a passage only Lucifer, or ones he wished, could find or enter. Beneath the pitch of hell, in his rooms there was light and a beauty to the place he dwelt when seeking isolation. The long corridor had a few candles when entered, then more, and halfway the candles were replaced by lamps that filled the way with soft light. At the end of the corridor were two doors. One small and locked from the outside, the other massive and made from wood he had carved.

His room, where he defiled virgins and did deeds that would never be spoken of, was filled with wooden chairs and tables, frame for his massive bed, cages to hold captives with wooden bars, torture racks and devices of all manner that only he knew how to use to inflict pain on innocents. They entered, but never left. None knew of such acts, but if they did, they would never ask as the answer would sicken them for eternity. With the vile nature of things there, the warm color of the wood and the lamps made the room comfortable and seductive.

"And when are you going to run out of tree? There is even more made from that wood than when I was called here before. I know you are proud, but using the tree from the Garden that Eve ate from? Is that not gloating? There are none who see it. Me, but it means nothing to me except you give yourself too much credit."

Laughing, he got the meaning, then he stopped cold and his eyes were fire.

"Was there any other serpent there? Any other that caused her to eat the forbidden apple? I didn't notice her craving any other. Certainly not Adam."

She was already tired of his grandiose opinion of himself, and she sought only to fuel his ire.

"If not you, any other would do if it came along. You were just handy, hanging there. You didn't tempt her, she used you. The women there grow tired of the same offering, and she was ready for new fruit, nothing more."

Fire blazed from his eyes.

"As if you know anything about it. She succumbed to my temptation."

Sitting on a wooden couch filled with pillows and silks, she smiled at him.

"See. Prideful. Who is the meaning of all temptation? Who is the one words such as lust and desire were made to describe? Me. None can resist me, but only the most pathetic desire you. I take the ones who I choose. The priests, the righteous, the holy, the husbands. Kings, pharaohs, wives, queens, and if I had been in the garden I would have taken both of them and left you hanging."

Vanishing from his eyes, the fire went to a stone hearth and lit tinder from the Tree. Lucifer's eyes turned to glowing blue as they were when he was in Heaven long ago, and he smiled.

"Talk of prideful!"

Nodding, she stared at him for a long while. Her deep brown eyes locked to his, hers pulling in the nature of him, his pouring it out to be taken. She closed her eyes, then opened them again, looking at him with a certainty he could have caught in his hands for it was more than a look, it was a Thing.

"No, not prideful. Ashamed."

Opening sparring finished, he understood what she said could only be true. She, from him, was a deceiver but only to ones commanded to take as harvest. To him or any other she only spoke true.

"Daughter, for you to be lust, desire, craving, the last gasp any see as your form is beyond what is known as beauty… It is only how you were made, and it took no doing of yours to be such a tasty morsel. Never forget that you are that because I made you that way. I know what temptation and desire is. I invented it, not you. I created you and I think you need to remember if I can make you temptation, which is only as I know what temptation is, and I can be that whenever I wish."

Lifting a red silk, sheer and exquisite in its making, she held it just under her eyes.

"I speak true, and with me there is no need to do other. You only know temptation because there really only is one true temptation. And you can't touch it."

Standing before her, arms crossed, he admired her. It was his intent when creating what else there would be beside him, she had the same nature to know where to inflict the most pain. She had reminded him that his only idea of temptation was Gloria, his Sweetness.

"Well, let's add intelligence to the gifts I gave you when made. You are right. Sweetness is my ideal and you are a fantasy of what I have always hoped she would be. Easy picking. Elsa, you were made to be low hanging fruit. No, not fallen on the ground or bruised in any way, but not hard to have for those I wish to corrupt. Sweetness is not low on the tree. She is the highest fruit on it. The only one on the top, unreachable. And do you know why being that high makes her the sweetest there will ever be?

Not insulted by anything he said, it was a truth she existed with. He didn't know that her personal standard for a mate was higher than his. He only knew the worker who harvested using a form he made. She lowered the veil.

"Of course. Being highest, she has no leaves over her and she is naked. Being highest, unable to reach, she is untouched. A virgin in thought and form. And there, she receives the most light from the Father, and that makes her the Holiest of all in Creation. His light shines on her first before any other. She has all Divinity, all Grace, and she is Glorious. But, Father, look at us. There is Gloria on top of all things wanted, then the tree with the Angels, then the ground with the Children He made wanting to go up or down on the tree. The sinners cling to the roots and reach to your domain. Down they go, deep into darkness where there is no beauty and no light to grow in. And under that darkness, under that hell, the abaddon you made your home, underneath rock bottom, there is the truest depth of despair and a place of no hope. This room. With you, and sadly, with me. You are the opposite of Gloria and why she will never open her legs to you. She will cut that pathetic serpent and feed it to your minions, but she will never want it, or you. Even if you could take her... Oh, what a sad conquest that would be. A deal with her, nothing more. To take the one who doesn't want you. Who would rather be nothing than look at you. That is pathetic. That's the real sin made the day you fell. Even the Children of God know that to want a child is pathetic. They have no defense and are easy takes. I know all about easy takes. That is what I do for you. Gather the weak that don't put up a fight. But, oh, father, have you noticed that not only has Gloria put up a fight? She is the one stronger than you. You are an easy take for her. Right now, she is finding a way to have her Blade be given the power to strike without being threatened. When the Father releases its power to her Will, she will put herself in this place under rock bottom, slice off that serpent and impale you with it. When it writhes in agony being in you, not hanging from you, it will beg for mercy and being kind, she will slice its head down the middle and watch it die as it fills you. Then she will take her Blade and start hacking you. Tongue. Fingers. Toes. Nose. Then limbs. You will lay there on the granite, still desperate to have her, and she will let you stay as crouches over you where her beauty will be right above you, and she will wait an eternity as you are so close to what you have craved while she suffered. Kneeling over your head, she will pray her thanks for your Father. Give praise to Him, not to you. Right there, so close you could stick out your tongue to taste her. To lick what you think is so sweet. Ah, and that is why she cast your tongue from you first. She leaves your eyes and ears. You can see her. Yes, see what Sweetness is. Imagine being in Union with her as no other has been, and not to be able to taste the sweetness. That close. She left your ears so you can hear her say you are doomed. And she doesn't stop. She will take as long to finish you as you have made her suffer. While you think of some way to be whole again, to take her, she prays thanks to Father for making her the one thing you will never have, and for a Blade that has no Will but hers. I can't be sure, but she may just leave you when she grows free of her pain. There, on the granite, unable to call out. I think I have a Knowing that if so, she will Will herself to me, and tell me it is my turn. That, Father, is what waits for you. Know that my vengeance will not be as kind as hers."

For the first time since Created, Lucifer was at a loss for words. What Elsa had said was so disturbing, he was both decimated and yet aroused to climax at the vision of Gloria naked above him and so close to her. He had cum dozens of times and his lower half was white with cum, as was the ground around him. Elsa was reclined in the pillows, her gaze never leaving him. He knew she saw how sad a creature he was. Regaining some thought and ability to speak, he just stood, covered in his perverse response.

"You think that you could possibly do worse to me than what you described my Sweetness doing?"

Slowly nodding, Elsa looked innocent and surprised he would ask such a question.

"Of course. She is made of light, and I darkness. I see you are enjoying the submission you will endure. Let me give you a bit more pleasure, then. She will tell me that it is my turn, and I will kiss her, as my love for her is true. A deep, long kiss of love. And I will caress her, touch all the beauty you longed to possess. Then I will come here. First, I will look at you. Oh, for a long time. Enjoy the Vision as it will be one I will share many times ahead. Since your only hold on me is this silver necklace, the serpent coiled around my neck that is your chain to hold me, I will take the handle from your hand. The one cast farthest from you when the Blade sliced it away. I'll take the chain off my neck and put it around yours. I will hold the handle and test it. Give it the slightest tug. And your torso will rise from the tug. I will admire how beautiful you look with it around your neck. Then, I will take all the parts cast from you and sew them back onto you. I am no seamstress, so it will not be a tidy mending, but you will be whole again. Arms, legs, feet, hands… A nose. But I think I'll cook up your tongue and eat it for I will be hungry after such labor. I won't want to hear you ever again, so you will have no need for it. Then I'll pull hard on the chain and you will rise and stand before me. Then, we will go for a walk. A good doggy following on its leash behind its master. I'll take you up to your cavern and open it for all to ascend to redemption. Dismantle your hell as you watch. That will be a chance for all to come and spit on you or do whatever they please. I have no idea what they may do, but worry not, you will not perish from some burns or slicing. I'll take care of you. Then I'll lead you to Earth and parade you through the streets as my little bitch pet. I'll watch you be humiliated. Pissed on, spat at, cursed, and laughed at. The mighty hasataan, now the bitch of a tiny woman who can barely lift a pussy cat. I'll offer them turns having at look at the stump where your serpent once was, like an attraction in a market where they watch freaks and oddities. Free, no price for admission as all there had paid far too much already. Then, when all the Children are tired of you, I'll take you to Heaven and leave you at the Arch. You will meet your maker, the Father. He will ask you if you are sorry. The rest, father, is up to you. Gloria will be there, floating naked in the air above you. I will join her, whispering secrets only I know, telling her that I doubt you will apologize for you are one sad fucker."

Frozen, he was stunned, a new sensation. He knew all she said could happen, and would be worse than she had described and he deserved that and much more. With all that, he could only admire himself for he had created her. He had made her to be a true satan.

Only Elsa could devise such a plan to hurt him beyond what any could ever imagine. He was in awe of her.

"For the first time ever, I bow. Not even I could devise such scathing punishment. You are truly my daughter. I can only tell you I think each is horrific, but it remains that each is equal as each denies me my Sweetness and means I will never have her. Bravo. You know how to hurt as much as you give pleasure. Good job! This is a marvelous day. I have learned what else there is. What else could be worse than me."

She nodded at him and gave her most charming smile.

"Hey, you sad fuck. Me."

Scroll Seven

Standing looking at the single white rosebud, Gloria was confused and saddened by it. Turning to look at the Creator, expression serious, her manner revealed her concern.

"Father, it is true it is the most stunning and beautiful flower in Your garden. Praise to You for making such a wonder. But... such beauty... alone. All by itself. It is sadness. It is everything I don't want to be. I am not saying it isn't accurate for I am that. Alone. I exist Knowing it is doom for any next to me, for they will be taken by Lucifer for no reason other than to hurt me. Yes, this flower? It is perfect. You have painted a masterpiece, but one so accurate it pains me to see. I am sure it will make any who see it sad even if they know not why."

Hugging the most wondrous Angel that had ever been, the Creator wept, telling her He felt that sadness each time He went to the white rosebud, and each time His tears flowed for love of it, and the flower has only been given His tears to nourish it. He told her now her father had joined him, and his tears were mingled with His, and it was the only flower that had grown from the love of them in such manner.

Releasing her, they looked at each other. It was a moment of understanding, sorrow, love, and He nodded at her, holding His hand out for her to take and lead her to His cabin outside the garden.

"It is bittersweet. Yes. Bitter, and sweet, I know. To be one so pure, so beautiful in spirit, yet be alone. And you are right. Any close to you will be taken by Lucifer to do more than hurt you, but to lure you to surrender to not have them harmed. Know this, I speak true. When I thought of all that exists, I was surprised as the Thought gave things their own Will. Their own nature. I had no Thought that was what I was doing, but it can only be that I intended it as I wanted each created to have a Will of it's own. I hadn't realized that with Will free to do what it wished, that any would want to do harm to others. It concerns Me as I created all things, so as Lucifer has told you, it is I who created all evil. Not him, for I created him. Gloria, look at Me."

Stopping, He took both her hands, and with a look of sadness she had never seen before, He said only two words to her.

"I'm sorry."

Hugging him, she knew it was never intended to be what it was. Creation was as much a mystery to Him as to all who existed. He bore the weight of creating what caused suffering. It was a burden that was beyond any knowing. As He felt compassion for her, she felt compassion for Him. He too suffered her pain, though few knew that. Her father did and had raised her to know that the Father had a sadness none could understand. She would ask again and again why the One, with the power over all things, didn't change it all. He would explain that to make one change, to control anything created, all existence would have to be changed. All things had been created to have their own Will. To change Free Will, each thing would have to be changed. He could not change only Lucifer. It would mean the end of all things. She would ask in such a matter, what could be done.

"Long have been the discussions I've had with Father about that. He asked me what I thought, for He could not change the Thought that made Lucifer. I said I had already answered. Not change Lucifer. Stop him from doing harm again. It is why the Blade was forged from the scythe in my hand on the day I went to witness the creation of abaddon. I was harvesting the field, scythe in hand, and as I descended that day, it changed to the Blade. He was tuned to my thoughts once in abaddon that I must have a way to protect myself or any other from the hasataan, so my scythe became light, and it is the power of light that can strike the darkness in your uncle. The light will blind the darkness he has become, and he will be no more. The Blade is to stop him, send his darkness away, but only if a threat to any Angel."

Remembering such teaching, it was why she rose from abaddon, brought Lucifer by allowing him to follow her, and to learn if she could draw him out, alone, with only the Blade in her hand and no others she loved near. She had seen he would face her alone, at the entry to Heaven, and being a wise Angel always, he knew to never cross the line and threaten or harm her. With no others there, it would be only her to confront him, and that was what she wanted to learn before speaking to the Father.

Reaching His little cabin in the evergreens, they sat on His porch looking out to a wondrous valley that preceded the rise of mountains, a stream, blue, running near the porch.

"Gloria, you can't hide your mind. Not because it's Me, for I do not look into your thoughts. That is not My way and would be wrong. I mean in every manner you hide nothing. Anger, joy, sadness. I look at you right now and see determination all over you. You want to tell Me something. Ah, more. You want Me to do something. No need to do anything other than ask. Tell Me, what do you want?"

Reaching behind her neck, from under her long blonde hair she took the Blade from where it rested on her form. With no danger, it was a simple handle with no blaze of light or form of a weapon. She laid it on the table where they ate pears and cherries from the grove near the cabin or played cards. Laying it on the table in front of Him, she left it there.

"This thing is useless. It was once needed, and true, it protects me from attack, and others in Heaven from the same, but that means nothing now. All know Lucifer and need no protection as they know what falling with him means. Father, know this. I speak true. This day, a change must be made. If not, I walk away for I am sure I will have no Wings and no longer be Guardian if such a change does not happen. If a change is made, I will fly from here, the True Archangel. The True Guardian. My father, oh, I love him so, he took this Blade and created the Arch. To do one thing. Protect me from the fate my mother suffered. Praise be to Michael, he saved me…"

Glowing, the Creator was feeling the very Joy felt when He created all things. Gloria was why there was Free Will, as strange as it was. Sitting there with Him, she was Free Will and why He could never change a thing made. She was magnificent. She was the Joy of Creation, the best that any could be. He waited to hear what she would ask.

"This is the day. Like the day all things were made. It is the day I perish to Lucifer's will, or become the True Archangel. This Blade must change to shine light to any, not only Lucifer. It must be the line between right and wrong, good and evil. A Blade that can cast light to darkness no matter who is dark, or where that darkness is. It must do my bidding as Guardian. I will never strike at good, but will vanquish all dark with it. I wish to strike Lucifer for what he has done, not just what he will do."

Everything she said was flawless in intent. She wished to stop hurt, harm, and stop evil from corrupting anyone. He sat, running through what that meant, and why He hadn't made it such from the time when it was first given to Michael. He looked at the Blade's handle, and then at Gloria. His look was frustration.

"You are the Holiest of Angels, child. What you say is the most loving wish there can be. I wonder if you know what you ask?"

Gloria's eyes grew wide.

"If You start philosophizing, or pull out Your deck of cards, I say now I will go wayward. I will be gone. I have said one or the other. I am not forcing Your hand, as you say in Your card game. I am telling You what I will do either way. I have no choice. It is what it is. I respect which You choose."

"Child, I have but asked you to consider that if given the power to strike before a sin is made. It is much more than stopping evil. It would make you…"

Flying back from pure Will off the porch, Gloria's Wings filled the entire valley, and she was in her armor, but did not take the Blade. She called out to Him.

"I said no philosophizing. I speak true. I have thought of what You asked. You think it will make me equal with you. The One who decides what is good or evil, decides who exists. Decide what is good and what isn't. To be as You. No. If that is what I wanted, I would have asked to be You. To be God. No, I asked to be a true Guardian. To protect, not only Avenge. That is not being God. That is being a Guardian. To guard all from evil. Play Your game, I am wayward, Guardian no longer."

Watching Gloria, her Wings filled the sky above all Heaven, then vanished as He saw her fall to the hovel where she lived with Michael, blonde hair trailing above her longer than even He could imagine. Smiling, she was the most marvelous of dreams. She was everything He admired and wished He could be.

Scroll Eight

Spreading her arms out to her sides, her descent slowed as she reached the dusty path between the pond and her home with Michael. She knew he would be out gathering fruit and grains and thought if he wondered what she was doing filling the sky above with her Wings, then letting each feather fly off to take flight as doves. He would be back soon, and she had much to do.

The hovel was made by Michael long before she came into being. It is where he and Ethereal began their existence of love, and where she was born, the first true Angel as she was born of Angels, not from the Will of the Father. Michael was a First Angel, made by the Creator from Thought. She was the First Angel, made from love. All said that made her the Holiest of Angels, and she felt honored to be thought of as that, but was not of her doing. The honor belonged to her mother and father. She was their love.

Knowing it was why Lucifer desired Union with her, being the Holiest, the most pure, and the most beautiful was her curse. She was an ideal, much like the Creator. Even without Lucifer, she would be revered, thought of as the Holiest, and so revered she would not be thought of as one to have Union with. She was a temple to pray before, not be inside of. Her Majesty, her Grace, her pure beauty made her unapproachable. None could think they could ever match her as a mate for she was beyond what all others were. She had no equal in the minds of all others. It would be like a lovely young Angel maiden walking up to the Creator and asking Him to join in Union and be mated. No such thing had ever been done, nor would it ever be tried.

Looking in a mirror, she saw how all that was not what she was. She was a young girl. Lonely, hurt, and sad. She longed for love, and with that thought she felt the sadness as never before. Even if a wonderful man was brave enough to ask her to join him in a walk, to even dream of her, he would face Lucifer in time and be eaten. Anyone she loved that went beyond the Arch would be

seized by Lucifer as call to her to save the poor soul. He sought
the moment when she defended someone else, not herself. It was
at that moment he would impale her and make her his thing. His
Sweetness. He would send her skyward impaled with the head
of the serpent sticking out her mouth, held where all in eternity
could see that even the Guardian had forsaken God, and gave
herself to hasataan. The power and the glory of having her would
make him beyond God. He would rule. He never wanted her
to love, to cherish, to be one with. He only wanted her to be a
First Angel mated to the True Angel, and the hasataan would be
the one in control of all Creation and would cast the Father to
nothingness.

None of that could ever be. It was why she went wayward and
renounced the Blade and was no longer Guardian that day. She
would find another way to stop Lucifer. He was too smart to be
vanquished by acts the Blade would strike for. He had to make
a threat or do harm, and he would never make such a mistake.
He had learned what a mistake was. The very word came from
his deciding to Fall, thinking Ethereal would have little Gloria in
hand, falling with him. That was his first and only mistake. He
would not make a mistake again.

Deciding she would be cast out of Heaven by the Father for being
a wayward child, she took a small basket and started collecting
her few possessions. The hovel was made of mud that had been
dried to form blocks, and had no adornment. It was simple and
had a place to sit and eat from a table and chairs Michael and
Lucifer had made soon after being created. There were two rooms
off the main room, each where there was a bed. One once was for
Michael and Ethereal, but now only for Michael. The other was
smaller, and had a simple bed that replaced the one when she was
little Gloria. She had grown so tall Michael had to make a new
one for her. There was a table where she had a hair brush that was
her mother's. It still had strands of her mother's long blonde hair.
Ethereal showed her how to brush and braid her hair when she was
still in Heaven, and Gloria had never used it since. The hair was

her mother's and she cherished it. Putting it in her basket, she took a small picture frame from the table. It had the only picture of her and Ethereal together. She was on her mother's knee, looking up to her, Ethereal looking down at her as she was still so little. They were laughing, facing each other, happy to be together. Ethereal was so beautiful. She wondered why all in Heaven thought her the most beautiful Angel. Ethereal was. She hoped one day she would become as beautiful as she had been. She put the picture and frame in her basket.

Setting the basket on the table, she looked at the small rock sitting there. It was the right size to fill her hand and worn smooth from touching it. It was just a rock like any other, but not like any other. When she was very little, Michael and Ethereal had taken her to the wondrous waterfall at the edge of Heaven. It was the place where all the rivers and streams flowed, and the water was all the Grace of those in Heaven, flowing to the waterfall. There, at the edge of Heaven, the ground stopped and the rest of Infinity began. An Angel would fall off if they went further, into the nothingness of all else that existed. It was where Lucifer led the many First Angels he deceived to fall from Heaven, and Ethereal fell there to save Gloria.

The waterfall didn't have a lake for the water that was the Grace of the Angels to collect. It cascaded down to all of eternity, sending Grace to all the endless places made during Creation. The first place that was filled with the Grace of that water was called Earth. The lump of rock first made by the Thought was washed in the water, filled with Grace, and the soil in the water as it flowed through Heaven traveled with it and made land from the soil, and there with water and soil, the Grace blessed it's new home. Life emerged from the soil. It was the first place the Creator traveled to in the beginning, and the life there came from His likeness. The Children of Earth were not Angels, they were unto themselves, made from the nature of Creation, not the Thought of the Creator.

On the visit to the waterfall long ago, when heading back to their

hovel, little Gloria picked up rocks and threw them into a creek
feeding the waterfall. Asking Michael if she could have a rock, he
picked one out for her, a nice one that was smooth and round,
taking both hands to carry. She treasured it and kept it by her bed
since that day. Holding it, she thought how without the Blade the
rock would be needed as she could throw it at Lucifer and hit his
sick head with it, sending him flying from her.

She put the rock in her basket.

Next came little notes Ethereal had written to her. Reminders
to visit her uncle and the Father. Recipes for salads and cooking
grains. Some that said she was loved, with just that message and
a bite mark into the soft paper, the way her mother signed all
the notes. With the first note, she watched Ethereal write it, a
message that Ethereal would be there for her, always. She picked
up the note, and bit the bottom edge, handing it to her. She
asked why she bit the paper. Ethereal smiled and told her it was
an impression, and she wanted to show Gloria the impression she
longed to make on her. Tears filled Gloria's eyes as her mother had
made an impression on her most profound. She was all Gloria
wished she could be. She had surrendered her existence to protect
her from Lucifer at the time of the fall.

Putting the notes into her basket, she closed her eyes.

"Mother, I know you are not in nothingness, for you live in me
now. I am going to protect all the way you protected me. That is
the impression you made on me. To give myself to protect others.
You were the first Guardian, Not Michael. Not me. I am only doing
what you taught me must be done. Thank you for saving me."

Finally, there was the small length of blue ribbon Ethereal had
worn to tie her hair back at times. She had given it to Gloria when
her hair had grown long, teaching her in the mirror how to tie the
ribbon and telling her she looked wonderful with it in her hair.
It held her hair back, and being so young she asked her mother
what else the ribbon was for. Ethereal said the ribbon was to hold

things together. Take things that are apart, gather them, then tie the ribbon around them. She said that as her mother, and having a husband and a daughter, she was like the ribbon and held them together. She would always be their ribbon and hold them that way.

Gloria rubbed the ribbon on her face and began sobbing. Even gone, Ethereal was still the ribbon that held them all together. Even while crying without stop, she took the ribbon and pulled her hair back, tying it as taught. Eyes opening, she heard the sound of Michaels breathing, and he was standing in the door to her room watching. Looking at the basket, and at her, he had a questioning look to show he wondered what she was doing.

Still sobbing, she understood his concern, and managed to speak.

"I am packing my belongings. Father, I must go. I have defied the Creator and have become a wayward child. I will not be cast out, I will leave. I've been waiting for you to say I love you, and goodbye."

He stared at her, shocked, not knowing what to say.

Gloria's eyes widened more, and she reached back and took the ribbon from her hair, then looked at it, then Michael, then gently circled it around her hand and put it in the basket. Without looking at Michael, she spoke out loud that she was not yet deserving to wear the ribbon for she held nothing together, not even them as she had to leave. She was not able to wear it yet.

Michael looked at her, and longed to sit next to her and hug her tight and saying she was far beyond deserving, this day more than ever. Respecting her feelings, he held himself from his emotions and let her have her moment. After putting the ribbon in the basket, she stood, and he left her room to go to his. He found a basket, one a bit larger. She followed him and asked him what he was doing.

"I'm going to pack my possessions. If you are leaving, I am leaving with you. If you are a wayward child, then I choose to be a wayward father. Come, help me. I don't want to leave anything."

Scroll Nine

Standing looking at Elsa, Lucifer realized what a true satan he had made. Elsa looked at him, shaking her head in disgust, saying there were many such tall, beautiful blondes that would satisfy his craving for such sweets. Wishing to show her that he knew of such delights, he would let her know why he was the hasataan and more than a fallen Angel. Crossing his arms in front of him, she saw he was Willing an answer to come.

Making no sound, the large wooden door opened and two young Earth woman peered in, making sure they had permission to enter. He spoke to them using only his thoughts, and they went to him, the door closing behind them. They were beautiful in form, just turning from girls to women. Naked, they were tall with no fat, flawless of skin and complexion, white as if they had never been in the Sun. Their curves were perfect, no lines where their ass met their legs, no hair on their mounds, and breasts almost not there. Their hair was blonde and long, Elsa knowing them each to be ones reminding him of the Sweetness although she know none could equal Gloria's Angelic beauty.

Elsa admired the bodies, and they were in a trance, not even knowing who or what they were. Elsa could make any human do such bidding, but thought it meant nothing for without craving and desire, it was meaningless to her. Only when ones not under any spell begged and pleased to lick or touch her did she allow any to do such. Her father had no such standard, and simply fantasized that the blondes were Gloria, and she understood he saw them as if a dream, nothing more.

Once viewed by Lucifer from all angles, they stood, one on each side of him, hands rubbing his arms and chest, looking at him with lust, licking at him, and worshiping him. He Willed a chair to slide up for him to sit on to continue talking to Elsa, and as he sat, the two moved between his legs in front of him, and began kissing the still placid serpent. Seeing he had settled down and was past his fantasy of Gloria, she knew they could talk about why he had called her to join him, a request that was seldom made. He looked at her.

"Would you like one of them to lick you? Say which. They are both pleasing."

Shaking her head, she just wanted to hear what he wanted and Will herself back to Thebes and do some writing. When she left she had just lit candles and opening scrolls to scribble on and had only written a few words when she was Willed to his chamber.

"All yours, father. I don't have a Gloria fantasy, so wasted on me. Can you get to the point of why you called me? I was writing and you interrupted me."

"Really, what were you writing?"

"Just memoirs. My encounters with the foolish pharaohs. How long are you going to let the idiot Nefertiti live? I am so bored watching over her. She's a total idiot. She thinks she's a god now. Can't you collect your due so I can go wander the desert or something more interesting?"

"Soon. I stick to the deal, you know that. I have plans for her, and all the sex is preparing her for her rather special place here. A bit of training, and she's ready, really, so glad you reminded me. Oh, these two blondes are from the North where it's cold and rocky. A perfect place for you next. I tell you, everyone there is blonde. The men are huge, and they are getting out of control. Making their own gods and even their own pretend hasataan. Some twerp calling himself Loki. And there is some dumb fuck with a hammer. The leader is one-eyed and has ravens as spies. I was okay with the nonsense, but using my raven guise? No. Stepping on my line. It did get me to sample these two. I've done a few thousand of them and I have a thing for blondes. Well, you know all that."

"Yes, I agree they are made to your liking. What do you do with them after you fucked them up?"

"That's a good question. At first, I thought to eat them, take their souls. Then, well, put them on some toys. I do that quite a bit, but just short of tearing them apart. No, after the raven news, I spoil them, like right now, giving them time with the true serpent. No man there will ever please them once I've done them. I had fifty of them in here earlier and went at them. Spoiled all of them for good. A few with red hair, which I must say was an interesting look for a change, but they weren't as good as I had hoped. So, I fuck them up where they'll be frigid bitches and wont even suck cock, that gets the blonde warriors so pissed they go off killing each other. You know the method. Done it most all places. This time, with the blondes, I at least have a bit to get lost in. With the fifty earlier, I had them all lay in a circle with their heads to each other and I slept on a bedding of blonde hair. Ah, it was tempting to keep them here, but there's lots more to reap. I keep these two here for cleaning up. But, daughter, I digress. I did want to tell you after Nef, and before the northern twits, I have a different plan for you. Get you some new skills. This will be a test to see if you live up to your claim of being the true temptation."

Glad to hear that her time with Nefertiti was nearing an end, she was looking forward to a change. The blonde northern fold sounded like nothing special, but better than being stuck in royal chambers for a hundred years. She looked at him, waiting, but he was watching the blonde heads bob up and down and he was rubbing their hair with his eyes glazing over. She decided to snap him out of Gloria fantasies and get her instructions.

"Fool yourself that's Gloria's hair after I Will myself away. What do you want me to do?"

His eyes opened, and he let the hair fall on his lap, it moving and swaying as they were working hard to please him. He looked at her and grew somber.

"This is one where you just do what I say, and it's not like Earth where you do what the fuck you want. You do an excellent job. Better than what I would order you to do, so don't misunderstand.

By T. Ulick   71

This is one where you don't know how things work, and it's not to harvest, it's something for me. Vengeance. There is no room for fucking things up. A take that is more than a human. Can you behave for a while?"

Staring at him, she laughed.

"If they have them, of course. What do you mean more than human? What are you talking about?"

Lucifer leaned his head back, and she saw him smiling. At first, she thought it was the blondes doing him so well, but that wasn't it. It was just up and down, nothing unusual. He tilted his head back down, smile still on his face.

"Elsa, this is the moment you were made for. You are ready, finally. All that craving for love in you, wanting someone to love? I put that there for what you are going to do. It will take all your sweet, innocent nature, your charm, your appealing form to a man to be protected and loved… All of that, but also it will be with someone who you will fall in love with. And I will let you. That's right. Not only me, and since I won't love you, you will feel loved for the first time, ever, which is why we are talking. It is powerful, and you have never been loved. And you will love him. I am sure of it. I know it. So, know this. Loving, being loved… I am able to turn that off. And, I can hurt you and the one you will be in love with. That chain can pull more than you here. It can pull anyone you love with you. If you love somebody, you will do anything for them. This will be your first love, well one who will love you back unlike me. To love him you will have to let him go to save him. If not, he'll suffer forever and won't have you which is what will happen, only he will suffer here, and know you brought him here to be on those racks over there, watching me fuck millions of innocents while he will never fuck you. Do you have any idea what I'm talking about?"

Confusing at it was, Elsa realized the message. She was to find a man she would love, he would love her, and at some point she'd have to break his heart and leave him. If she loved him, that would break her heart too. If she didn't leave, he'd suffer more than both of their hearts being broken. It was so cruel, and she expected no less from him as he was cruelty. How could it be other?

"Oh, I get the idea. Find a good man, be the sweet thing I actually am inside but have had to hide or be choked and pulled back to the abaddon for me alone, make him fall in love with me, and I'll finally be allowed to use the love you put in me, then I have to leave him when he's most in love… when I'm most in love, as he'll be able to know that as it's my first time being loved. So, break his heart, and mine. That, or you pull him here and he suffers much worse than a broken heart. Is that what you are trying to tell me. Oh, I can see it is…"

As she summed it all up, hearing the last sentence, she heard the two girls choking and gagging. He had erupted in them. He enjoyed hearing her talk about her heart being broken. The two blondes turned and looked at Elsa, their faces proved his delight even hearing her speak of it.

"Yes, you notice that I found your understanding, well, quite exciting. Hold on a second… You two, I will want more later."

He waved them away, the large door closing behind them. He leaned forward and his eyes were on fire once again.

"This is very simple. It's something only you can do. Go to Heaven. You aren't Angel or Demon so you are free to enter. I have a map for you of where to go. You will go to a grove of apple trees that have branches higher than you can reach. It's why I made you so small. Reach for an apple, and stick your breasts out, arch your back and get that sweet ass out like it's about to eat dick, and a man will be walking to the trees, see you, and offer to help you. Simple as that. You just say you are hungry, and Elsa, he will know if you are lying. You are hungry, indeed. For love. Take the apple he gives you, take a bite, then with your pretty little mouth shaped bite on the apple, offer to share it, and let him take a bite. It will all happen from there. He will love you, and you will love him. Be honest, say you are there to take him, seduce him, betray him. Do not lie. He will not lie to you. And tell him the truth you are controlled by me, hate me, and the chain around your neck is how I will pull you back. Amazing, isn't it? I'm asking you to love, tell the truth, and beg for his help saving you. No deception. No using your temptation. You are wonderful without all of that. Much more desirable without it. I was sure of this when I made you. You are a sweet, innocent thing with a vicious motherfucker father. We both know that. Let's see how you do just being you. Now, isn't that something? After the hard task of having Nef's tongue up your ass each night, my little reward for you. I need a break from being such a fucker sometimes. Look how nice I let those blondes do me? Sweet, kind to them. A chance to be loving and decent helps me know what truly evil is. You will learn much from this. Do you understand? Can you see that I'm rewarding you? You are my daughter, and I do care about you. There, a secret that I'll never reveal again. We will leave now and I'll reap the Nef bitch in, then you can take this little break. Sound good? Any questions?"

It was all unexpected, but the strange thing is that being an Angel, he was made to speak true. He had never told her anything that was not true. As sick as it all was, he always did what he said. He was her father, and he was insane, but he seemed to have a plan for her that called on her very nature and need for love. Even a demon needs an incentive to keep doing such work. She had no choice, regardless. She could only speak true.

"I know what is wanted, and yes, I can do that. I only have one question. You said it was in Heaven. I know I can enter, and you have it all mapped out. The question is only who is the man?"

Jerking himself off while he said all his instructions, not unusual as he was usually jerking off if no human woman were there, he came as he told her who she was to meet.

"Michael. My brother. Gloria's father."

Scroll Ten

Finding his own sentimental treasures, Gloria was crying at the love Michael had shown and the faith he had in her. He smiled at her, saying he was shocked she thought he would let her go and not be with her. He was her father, and they were held together by that ribbon as it was love. She hugged him tighter than she ever had, and he could feel the love she had for him flow from her into his soul. He loved her for every reason possible, but most of all because she was who she was. A caring, loving soul. She was worthy of all the praises she was given, but she was not in need of any of those. He knew she would be happy to just be a young woman with a mother and father and a simple life at home. She had never wanted more than that. Being a Guardian was something that she needed to be, not wanted to be. It was to honor her parents and let no others suffer such a loss as they both had endured. She was his daughter, and that's all he ever wanted her to be. Having the Blade and being a warrior was never something he wanted for her, but they both were warriors now, and she was the true Guardian.

As she squeezed him tight, he opened his eyes and in the doorway to the hovel stood the Creator, with a small basket of his own, waiting for them to notice Him.

Michael leaned up to whisper in Gloria's ear, a long reach for she was taller than him, telling her the Father was at the door. He felt her jump as she let him go, turning first to look at him in panic, then shouting out to the Father she was busy packing her little things and would soon be gone as any wayward child must do. Michael smiled once more, admiring her reaction, but he knew that the Father was not there to banish her. He was smiling, and they both nodded at each other.

"Father, you know Gloria is prone to be dramatic. She is just that way. Let's indulge her a bit, and that will make what You say mean even more."

Nodding with delight, the Father stood in the door, and Micheal went to stand with Him. They stood and watched Gloria running about, finding the rest of Michaels possessions and putting them in his basket. He decided to tell the Father of their plans.

"I have news most sad. Gloria has told me she must leave as she will not wish to be cast out. I could only speak true. I said if she is wayward, I must be too, for I am her father and will be with her in all things. She is gathering my personal treasures then we will be a burden no longer."

Speaking loud enough for Gloria to hear, she added that being wayward ran in their family. Even her mother went wayward and fell to do the right thing. If that is what must be done, she will honor her wayward mother; Michael will do the same. The Father smiled at Michael, letting his thoughts know he must be the proudest Angel in all Heaven to have such a wonderful daughter. Michael nodded. That was true. He watched as the Father moved to the large table and pulled out a chair, calling out to Gloria.

"If you have time, will you sit with Me for a bit before you fly away?"

Looking up from under her father's bed, Gloria looked surprised, then worried.

"Do you plan more than to banish me? Are you here to unleash your wrath? Your ire? Oh, Michael, you have done no wrong! Flee!"

The Father spoke to Michael's thoughts.

"Wrath? Ire? Flee? Yes, she is prone to dramatics!"

Michael smiled, nodding. The Father called out to Gloria.

"Things will be much better if you indulge me. Gloria, if you join me, there will be no wrath or, what was that you said? Ire? No, none of that. I speak true."

Looking cautious, He declared He spoke true, and that must be respected. She stood up, flattened her linen sheath and straightened her hair. Walking to the table, Michael had taken a seat after pulling one out for her across from the Father. Gloria was visibly worried, but was doing her best. She had missed a long strand of hair and it fell in front of her face, and she blew at it with no result, then batted at it which put it in place. She put both hands on the table, sat upright, and looked at each of them, then right at the Father. He looked at her with a serious expression.

"Gloria. You trouble my mind. Truly. We must talk."

Her eyes widened, and it was clear she was readying herself for the worst.

"Father, your troubles will soon fly away. If that is not enough, and you wish to talk, then please, no smiting or thunder. No vengeance need be unleashed. I understand I was rude and gave You an ultimatum. You have always been kind and loving to me, and I was the one filled with ire, but not for You, for the true wayward child. You know who."

Keeping his serious manner, Michael knew it would be hard to maintain, so he helped the Father a bit.

"Gloria, you didn't mention being rude or ultimatums. Did you do that?"

"Yes, I can only speak true. I laid my Blade down, I surrendered my place as Guardian, and took off before he could smote me! Fast as my little Wings would carry me!"

Unable to stop himself, Michael burst out laughing, and the Father looked at him and joined him. Michael managed to stop laughing long enough to speak.

"Little Wings? Little? Gloria, you had them filling the sky for all of Heaven to see. I don't think of that as them being little! And what of the dramatic fall when you let them fly from you? I think everyone saw that as well. I did."

"Father, you know that's hardly how large they can be. They can fill eternity if needed. What, all in Heaven just happened to be looking up to the sky that moment? They've seen me take flight many times."

Her eyes rolling up to the boards holding the grasses on the roof above her, she waited to see if Michael would give her some support on her flight being not as attention getting as he claimed. He was still laughing as he turned to the Father, knowing she would be watching.

"Father, did she do all of that? Really? Pushed the Blade to you? Flew off before You could philosophize? Well, that must be a first. Who has ever done that? Not even my brother. He just ran off without challenging you."

"Father! I am your little girl. How can you hurl such scurrilous accusations at me?"

Gloria looked at Michael, and he could see she was serious.

"Scurrilous? Gloria, where are you coming up with these terms? Where did you learn those?"

"Oh, as if that's hard to figure out! When you have Lucifer on your tail, you learn much. Anyway, look on the shelf over there. A dictionary from Earth. I've been reading it."

The Father patted Michael's shoulder, then Gloria's hands. He smiled at her. There was no way to keep from laughing as she was being fully serious. He wanted her to know what He was feeling.

Angel

"Gloria, you are someone who amazes Me more each time I see you. I admire you, and I was proud of you. It is true none have ever stood up to Me or defied Me. The amazing thing is that I never told anyone they couldn't! I have never had cause to share this, but I want to tell you about why some may worry about telling Me they don't agree with something. I want to share it with you, and your father. I promise no wrath or anything. I speak true. Can you honor Me by hearing Me speak without My philosophizing?"

Clearly relaxing and letting down her guard, she smiled at both, and her smile answered all questions. No words were needed.

"Gloria, just seeing you smile lifts Me higher than Wings could ever do. That's what I needed right now. Thank you. I am not vengeful. Wordy, yes. I know many things, and one is that even when a person is sorry, truly sorry, the person who is hurt can forgive, but it doesn't mean they can forget. When a person is hurt, that hurt changes many things inside them. Some hurts can't be healed. I know you understand this, for you will never forget the pain of losing your mother. Your father won't, and I will never be without the pain of that, for I feel responsible. No, no need to say it wasn't My fault. Please, I will let you know why what you did today changed Me, and why I am amazed by you. I brought some of your favorite fruit to thank you. Please, enjoy some while I explain."

Looking at the basket, Gloria asked if there were apricots, them smiled as the Father reached into the basket and took several out for all of them. She nodded at Him, and started eating the succulent pick as He continued.

"When Lucifer grew more insane, I, like all others, had no Knowing of such a thing. None had ever gone insane before. Even worse, he locked on to a thing I said that was a hope for him, that a mate would show up, and I tried to calm his worries saying she would be a sweet one. Now, the fruit we are all eating, each one is wonderful, and they are indeed sweet and delicious. Agree?

Ah, no need to say it, I see your nods say more than words. Like this basket of sweet fruit, confused as to why no mate appeared for Lucifer, I was confused and understood he felt excluded and different. It was the same as if I planned to have him visit and said there would be fruit, most sweet like these apricots, for him when he arrived. There are many apricots, and they are all sweet. I meant that when his intended mate arrived, I was sure like all Angels that day, she would be sweet. A sweetness he would love. Nothing more. I had no way to know who, or when. I think it was a hope, but I know he took it as a promise and that I knew who his sweet love would be. I didn't. I ask, would you hear it different than I intended, I mean if I had been speaking to you?"

Michael looked at Gloria, indicating he had an answer.

"Father, I was there, and heard what You said. I can only speak true for myself, but I did speak to Ethereal and she shared my reaction. It was all new, and we were new that day. It was new to You as well. Two things happened and it is why Ethereal and I talked about it many times. First, of all the Angels made that day, Lucifer was the only one alone. We empathized how that must have felt for him, and we felt sadness as he clearly was hurt. The second thing is that being new, we thought all things must be for a reason, and understood You wanted him to not feel hurt, or left alone, so wanted to reassure him with a comforting message that one will be for him, if not that day, another. We both understood that You meant all things being new, all Angels being most wonderful and it is true, loving and sweet in nature, that You were saying a sweet Angel would arrive for him and not to worry. It was reassurance, but we did not think You knew who or when. But we could see he thought You did. I never heard other Angels say when is the sweet one You knew of going to arrive. Only Lucifer thought that in our way of Knowing."

Looking sad, the Father patted his shoulder again, nodding.

"That was what happened, and now I am Knowing. It was a mistake to say that."

Michael shook his head, saying he thought it was a kindness, not a mistake. How could it be other?

"It was. All turned to Me as the Father, something I was not aware that I was. It was thought that I know or controlled all things, and you both know that I have given all things their own nature and Will. I was not Knowing of all that on that day. But I was wise in other things. On Earth, when new, I would visit. The place was lush with trees, and I marveled at the patterns they formed. I learned something about the nature of things. In a grove of trees there is an order, and it may look random to most, but I could see the pattern. Healthy trees grow in a way where their roots mingle, and they talk to each other and share nutrients. It is why trees grow in groves or forests. They are a family. Then I began to see trees that were not in the pattern. Ones growing alone, or outside of the root system. Those trees were different, and most never grew properly. Being alone, seeking the Sun, they looked different. Strange. They would die or grow ill. Then, I noticed that with most all living things. Small insects, birds. A nest could be full of birds with beaks wide for their first meal, but one not like the others, head down, not wanting to eat. It too was troubled. Sometimes, as it grew, it would attack the others in the nest, stealing their food, never getting its own. I had no answer, but knew that in the nature of living things, there were often ones different enough to reason that something wasn't right. That they were against their very nature though it was no fault of their own. It happened. They rarely fared well. I tried to save such ones, but they did best on their own, many times happiest when apart as they knew they were different."

Taking out cherries from the basket, all delighted for they were also favorites. The Father ate some, and nodded that they were wonderful.

"Ah, the way I see cherries now… It is a memory that is troubling, and you will learn why soon. Back to the day when I attempted to reassure Lucifer, inside I had a Thought that there was a bird

in the nest different from the others. A tree off from the grove. I
had a worry of that but did not think that the Angels were such. I
thought no more than there would be more and more Angels and
one would be there for him. I was wrong. That is my Knowing,
now. The nature of things tells us what is needed. The fact that
thousands of Angels appeared hand-in-hand, mated, but Lucifer
was alone was a clear message that he was different. My telling
one so different that he would be the same, soon, was a terrible
mistake, and Gloria, that is what I want you to know. I was wrong
to plant a seed where it must not grow. He was not one to have
a mate, for he was not like any other. Not that each should ever
be the same. That is not what I mean. I mean he was not part
of all that was that day. He was the tree alone. Being smart, he
felt different and told me that in many ways. His expressions,
his worry. He was feeling alone that very day. Even taking my
comforting as a promise, or that I had one in mind for him was
a sign. Even as he grew to learn the way of the nature of things,
he clung to that one thing I said, even knowing that some Angels
chose mates on their own, and not all arrived mated. I saw the
difference in him over and over, and hoped it would be where he
grew past worry and to understand nothing was more than he was
different, as each of us are. It was that he was far more different.
Michael, I have a hard question for you, and I ask only that you
speak true. This is very hard. You have watched all here arrive,
and all the ones born as Angel Children. They are wondrous and
like all Angels, beautiful from birth. You have seen most all the
young Angel girls grow. From young girls to young women to full
women. Please, this is important for me to know. In all those you
saw, did any stand out where you looked at them and had some
emotion seeing them? Any thought that you would love to know
them or be closer to them in a loving way?"

Gloria looked shocked, ready to defend Michael. He held up
his hand, telling her that was an important question and he
understood why it was asked. She had comfort in his assurance,
and relaxed.

"I have looked at all I've known, and I would think of how

beautiful they were, or how attractive they were. When I told Ethereal I saw a young daughter of a friend, I would tell her the girl was beautiful, and would attract many as she grew. There is a line between recognizing someone's form is attractive — and being attracted to them. When I saw any attractive girl or woman, I knew she was beautiful, but I had no attraction to them. No desire to be with them as more than a friend of the family or such. No lust or craving or thoughts of them. I was attracted to Ethereal. I knew, and know the difference. If I had ever had an attraction for a young girl, I would have went to you and asked how could that be? That would be something was not right. I hope that I explained that in a way that makes sense."

Looking at Gloria, Father asked her if she understood what Michael meant. She nodded.

"Yes. Of course. I have seen all here, and because I see a boy who is handsome I know he is, but that just is what is. I will explain a bit more than Michael has. I can see a man and I think that he is most attractive and understand why his wife thinks special of him. They have an attraction to each other and that is why they are together. I would be worried if I looked at a little boy and had the same reaction. Thinking that the little boy is attractive and I would love to be close to him. That is not what I think when I see a handsome young boy. I know that all Angels here look at me and think me beautiful. I worry sometimes, and Father, forgive me as this is prideful, but I think about what if my beauty is such that the husbands or boyfriends think I'm more beautiful then their chosen one? Or, and this is very troubling, what if they think of me when holding their mated one? Thinking I am in their arms to excite them. I don't want that, but I think that worry is natural as we are not able to understand why we are attracted to a person. The mating has to be right, or that could happen and I don't want to ever be the one who any is compared to."

She shook her head and started crying.

"Father, please, I ask this of you and need to know. It worries me. I have lived with being lusted by Lucifer because I am beautiful. Only you know, and you do not have to say who, but are there others who think of me, this form that I have, when making love to their mate? Please, tell me. Am I a wanton hussy? A home wrecker?"

Crying even more, she was sobbing. Michael began to reach to her, but the Father put his hand up to let him know only He could answer. He waited, and Gloria put her head up, a look of pleading on her face as she waited for an answer.

"Gloria, again, you amaze me. This is what makes you the Holiest of all Angels. To worry that is loving and reveals your nature. I am also amazed at what terms you have gleamed from that dictionary. I digress... I will answer, and I can only ever speak true. The answer is not easy to say or hear. It is one to understand, and it has taken me much thought to be right in My mind. Gloria, when it comes to love and Union, all, and I mean Angels and Children, go through trials and have irrational thoughts. To answer you, yes, there have been many men who love their wives who find themselves thinking of you and your form. Don't panic, please. This must be learned, just as I had to learn it. There is a word I mentioned. Trial. And as your father mentioned, there is a line between action and thoughts. I have talked to men, so in love with their wives or intended, who come to me or pray to me that they were in the arms of their love and for no reason, thought of you in their arms..."

Gloria cried out, a scream, crying it was true, she was a heathen temptress! She put both hands to the sides of her face, then saying no, no, over and over. The Father held his hand for Michael again, telling him to have faith in his daughter. He waited, then told Gloria to look at him. She could only do what He asked for He had been asked to answer her question and knew it was something important to her.

"Gloria, I have told you the most intimate, difficult thing those men have endured. Enough to confess it to me and turn to me for help. I spoke of a trial. They were being tested. All made, even me, have doubt and are unsure of things sometimes, most often about loves. I have told you what I have told no one else. I have told you that men thought of you when making love to their true loves. Gloria, this is amazing. This is the Knowing of the Father. Let Me ask you, have any men, and I do not include Lucifer, ever approached you to go talk to them? Express desire for you? Look at you with longing or lust?"

"No. Not that. No, never."

"And I will ask one more question. Do you ever have a thought you don't want? Something that shouldn't really be in your thoughts. You don't have to say what such a thought is about, only if you have had thoughts that you didn't want In your mind?"

Sitting, Gloria began trembling. Michael didn't wait, he reached for her hand, holding it. He said she was in a place of understanding and love. There was nothing to be ashamed of. She looked at him, then nodded. She turned to the Father.

"Yes, I have."

"Gloria, you can become more than you ever have been. I will not ask of any such thoughts to explain but for one. You did have one today, didn't you?"

She began shaking and crying, saying yes, yes, over and over. Then she stopped, and looked at the Father.

"Yes. Today. When telling You not to answer me with philosophy, and you started doing it. In my mind was how stupid you were!"

With that, she was in hysterics, and fell to the floor, wailing. They heard her saying, then screaming,

"I thought you were stupid and meant it!"

The wailing was beyond anything they could have imagined. Michael looked to the Father, and He nodded, got up and went to Gloria who was thrashing on the floor in despair. He knelt down and leaned to put his mouth over her ear. Though said as a whisper, He knew Michael could hear.

"Gloria, sometimes I am."

Her head turned to him, and she stared into His eyes, and He nodded.

"And Gloria, as you flew off, I don't know why, but the words in My thoughts said, "Spoiled brat!"

They stared at each other, and neither knowing why, each broke out into hysterical laughter. She reached up to hug him, saying "Hold me, stupid!" He held her with all his love, answering, "Anything to keep the little brat quiet!" She started pushing him in jest, him pushing back. Finally, they made it to their feet to go back in their chairs. Michael was sitting with a look of confusion. The Father asked him to speak. Michael looked at Gloria, then to Him.

"Little? Again, little? Now, there is an irrational thought!"

That had them all in hysterics. Throwing cherries at Michael and Gloria, the Father said that was wonderful.

"Oh, I am so happy right now. Thank you, Gloria. Thank you. I've been wanting to say that for so long!"

Nodding, looking Him right in his eyes, she answered.

"So have I."

He smiled at her with a love that would never leave her. He nodded again.

"That was completely, wonderfully normal. We all think things like that, but we don't act on them. We don't say it because it's just a reaction to a moment or something said. So, the men who thought of you? When they did, they stopped and thought about why they would think that. And the answer was that they were being tested in some way. It doesn't make sense. Then, they looked at their love, and it was then they saw her as the most beautiful one ever made. They knew that they were with the one who was beauty for them. Love and attraction is to the spirit, the soul, not the form. Thinking of your form helped them understand why they were in love with the one they held. It was irrational, but those trials, those moments, we learn from them. Gloria, speak true. Do you think I'm stupid?"

Smiling, she said of course not. She thought him far smarter than even when he was standing in the door. He told her that it was no secret she was spoiled, but he didn't think she was a brat. Far from it, after telling of her worry for men who thought of her form, that was as far from a brat as she could be.

Feigning innocence, Gloria looked at him and said, "Spoiled? My father says he'll do anything for me. Even go wayward for me. And you think I'm spoiled? I know I have been. By both of you. You see what I've faced with my sick uncle and have been too kind to me. I know that. And that has helped me get through things many times. Thank you. Both."

"It is good to know who and what we are, Gloria. I know you do know yourself. But that brings us back to Lucifer. He challenged Me, but not the way you did today. Visiting me one day, he said that he wished to have his own domain. I will admit I knew the word, but had never heard it used, so asked what he meant. There was a strange look in his eyes, again, something I knew could be but had never seen. Explaining what he meant, he wished to leave and be free from Me. That is how it was said."

Looking at Michael, Gloria asked if he had been told of such intent. Shrugging, Michael said only that Lucifer had been telling Ethereal he was thinking of making a new place where Angels could build their own heaven of sorts. I thought it philosophizing, but learned all too soon it wasn't. He was serious. Father, I never knew what he said to You. Was he insulting You?"

"Ah, the words. Insulting. There was no such word before the fall, but now I know that he was being so. I asked was he not happy, here in this place. Shaking his head, he said he wasn't. I asked what was meant by his own domain. He grinned, saying a place without Me. Where all were free to do as they wished. I know he was unlike other Angels, but it was… Well, something I had no idea of. He was hiding his thoughts and feelings. It was a surprise."

Sadness fell on the three, each looking at each other, knowing where his discontent led. The fall. It was the beginning of pain and suffering for those who followed Lucifer. Michael asked if He thought it would be a good place, a way to be independent but still live in Grace.

"No, Michael, he was hiding his intent, but I could see he wished to live different than all here. No, a state of what we know as sin. I say it was insulting as he came and asked Me what I thought. Now, I see he was testing Me to learn if I had any notion of his plan. Perhaps more so if I would try to stop him. He asked next if I would prevent him from going, or taking others who wished to follow him from leaving. It was a surprise, and I only had one question. Asking where would he go, for there was only one Heaven. I asked if he meant a place like Earth, for that was for Children, not Angels. Looking into his eyes, I could see he had no plan to share. All I could do is say he was gifted with Free Will. All Angels were. If he wished to leave, and take others with, I would respect his choice. His Will. I still question if that was wise, but I know it was. If not in abaddon, he would have made Heaven into his hell."

Gloria grew somber, and putting her hand out in front of Michael, letting him know she wished to speak without interruption, he nodded.

"Father, you are Knowing of your little Wayward Angel…"

Wanting to question her describing herself as little, Michael resisted the question and let her continue.

"You know of my intent by my actions, and it is true, I am willing to tell You if I see the path ahead needing change. Lucifer had been a different one since created. Didn't You know? He never pursued a mate or a love, but I have learned from many that looking at me since I was little Gloria, his eyes lit when he saw me. It was desire. Didn't You see that? Know that? The fall was a ruse to take me for his sick needs, and You had no idea?"

Growing sadder, the Father slowly shook His head, and looked into Gloria's eyes to touch her very existence.

"There is a saying the Children of Earth have. All is easy to see looking back. Hindsight. Gloria, no. I knew nothing more than he delighted in you. I thought it love for you, and that is what he showed, ever. It was deception, never true. Now, knowing of the assurance he would be mated with the sweetest Angel, and knowing that you were the most holy, the first true Angel, I failed you. I didn't put that together with all that followed. It was new. Nothing before that time would have Me thinking such sickness was in him. He is truly a great deceiver. He deceived Me."

Even hearing such admission, Gloria was relentless for her whole existence turned to sorrow on that Knowing. Her mother sacrificed herself for her, her father became a warrior where he was once only gentle. She had never been able to find love or a mate for fear that Lucifer would take him to pull her from safety. She continued to stare at the Father.

"Father. I ask that You speak true. It will not change my love for You if you answer in a way that is sad. You respect Free Will and will not interfere with the Will of any. So, again, speak only true. If Lucifer had said he wished to leave Heaven, take me, and have his way with me where he was free of Heaven, would You have stopped him?"

Michael watched them both, knowing it was a moment much like the day Lucifer fell. A moment that would change all existence. Not as Lucifer had for sickness or evil, but that the Free Will of another could be challenged — or choice altered by force. He knew the answer she would get, and he was filled with sadness for it would change the nature of all things.

"Gloria. I speak true. No."

Promising she would love Him no matter what He answered, she thanked Him for speaking true. Leaning back, she looked at Michael, her look assuring him she would accept the truth for it was sincere and held no intent to harm her, then or now. Both watched her as she nodded at the Father.

"Father, I respect You more than ever, for that was a hard thing to say to Your little one, the one who lives the pain of Free Will each moment. But I speak true. It is the answer I needed to hear. I will do as Lucifer did and go against the order of things and change all things to come. I have made no secret of my intent, where he did. I ask that as you supported Lucifer's intent, that You support mine. I will say exactly what that is, and what I need. It is what I declared earlier when I took Wing. It is what I will do, not an idea and I am not asking Your permission as yes, I have Free Will. Know this. I will use it. I will stop any who intend to harm any other, or have harmed them and plan to harm more. I will stop the Will to harm. I will prevent them from doing harm to any others. To do that, I ask you to let me use the Blade to stop evil, not just once done, before it takes place."

Knowing what she was asking, and also knowing the Father knew she wished no opinion from Him, she only wished to have a weapon that respected her Will, her judgment. It was something new. She would be a true Guardian. Guarding any from harm, not avenging harm done. The Father had no hesitation in His reply.

"Gloria, you are truly glorious. I have thought on what you ask, and I respect your Will, and more, think it is that of a true Guardian. I will not stop any's Will. Be the Guardian you are. I will do this as you need to protect yourself from Lucifer. I ask you leave the Blade of Divinity with your father. The ones here will continue to need protection from him, or his followers. The Blade of Divinity is not powered by Me. It is the power of your father's Will. Now, yours. Leave it for him. He didn't have to ask me for his scythe to become the Blade. It was his Will. Gloria, you have your Will to have a Blade that guards. You only need to Will such a weapon to be. What is that, behind your neck?"

Looking at the Father with confusion, all she could do is reach under her hair and see what he meant. Michael felt the Blade of Divinity resting in his belt. He marveled at Gloria's face as she took a Blade handle from under her hair. Looking at it, then to him, then the Father, she said nothing. Standing up, she held the strange new Blade handle up, and though no evil was there, she gave it the Will to become a full Blade. It blazed with a might that shook the hovel. Glowing with a pure white fire, it was as long as she was tall, and it hummed with the power of the Will inside of her, which was far beyond what the Blade of Divinity had when used.

Realizing the Blade was more than just mighty, it ignited with only her wish for it to fire. It would fire when she wished, not only once harm had been done. It was new. It was under her control.

Standing with the Blade raised straight above her, she spun

around with the white light making a circular disk of fire that was near as large as the room. Just as quickly as it fired, it stopped. She put it behind her neck, then went to the Father, hugged him, and asked him what it was named.

"Gloria. It has a name for what it is. The Blade of Glory. It is you. Your Will. Your might. It will do what is right, for you are the meaning of the word righteous. It will never harm any not about to do harm as you would never do such."

Her sheath, a simple linen of white, changed to white crystal, clear in nature, but formed to her as a second skin. It was her Will and would shield her from any evil intent. Michael looked at her and knew her as a warrior like no other. She looked like none had ever looked. Something to be feared. Mighty. Powerful. She was all that, and still the sweet child he raised. The Father looked at her, then asked her one of the most amazing questions Michael had ever heard.

"Gloria, there is no evil here. Isn't it time to protect those in need of your Will to stop innocence from being taken away?"

Smiling, Gloria looked more beautiful than anything in all Creation. She was glorious, and the Guardian for all goodness. She gave Michael a kiss, then the Father.

"I will after I do one thing. Please, both, come with me to the Arch."

In that instant, the three were standing at the Arch. Not sure what Gloria would do, she stood back from them and in front of the line in the sand that prevented evil from entering Heaven, she looked at them, then down to it. Taking her Blade, it fired. Holding it pointed down to the path, with a might never seen, she drew a line. Putting her Blade back behind her neck, she stood with her arms out, looking to the Heavens, and in a voice that filled all creation, declared there was a new line.

"To all who harm any, know this day there is a new line in the sand. The line between good and bad. Cross the line to do harm to any, you will know me. Gloria. The Guardian."

Scroll Eleven

All around Lucifer began shaking, and the black granite of all abaddon was trembling, cracking, black dust filling the cavern and Lucifer's chamber. Hearing wailing from not only the caverns above him, he also heard wailing from the Children of Earth. Such had never happened before and he knew it was not a force of nature for there was no nature to abaddon.

Willing himself to the cavern above his chambers, spires and hanging stalactites were crumbling, the granite ground cracking open, and in the large space with its dome having a gigantic hole where lost souls poured in from Earth, he heard the last words trumpeted by Gloria declaring any who do harm would know her, the Guardian. Raising his arms like a bird about to take flight, he vanished as he cared not what happened to any there. He did not head to Heaven or anyplace where he would find Gloria, for he knew what she meant. She had not called herself the ArchAngel, nor even Angel. Just the Guardian. Understanding the meaning, it meant she was no longer bound by the respect for those who had yet sinned, only threatening it or thinking it. Of all sinners, he was the one she would strike first. He was no longer safe in abaddon, or anywhere in the realm of existence.

Only Elsa, his daughter, knew of the true abaddon. It was not a place in the material universe, and it had no shape or form, no substance or matter. She was created in the abaddon none knew how to reach, a Knowing she wished she had no knowledge of for it was the mind of Lucifer.

Her father was something new, not known before, and she was new in that she was a soul but not from Creation or birth. She was made from the Will of Lucifer, just as he had been made from the Will of God. She came into being by the power of his thoughts and determination to be mightier than his Creator, and had succeeded in creating her with life, soul, and existence. She was the only one of her kind. Made by the son, not the Father. She was not an Angel, demon, or Child of Earth.

To create her, Lucifer had created a place where only he, and then Elsa, could go. Into his insanity. His mind. When he wished, he Willed himself there, and to any near, he imploded into himself. His form was pulled into his mind and at that moment he was what may be called pure thought, but it was pure insanity as he was insane. It was where he created Elsa, and where he would send her if she disobeyed him, for she was but a thought he had, made real in his mind.

Opening her eyes from a state of nothingness, she was fully grown, never an infant or child. She was beauty beyond imagination, had knowledge equal to all Angels and Lucifer himself. She knew she was an idea that came into being and she knew she was from his mind and madness. His mind was an endless swirl of sand, ever moving, ever changing. Above was sand, not a sky, and there was no beginning or end to the desert she awoke in. Kneeling in the sands of his insanity, the place was ever changing, as were his ideas. As she knelt, she learned that she too was like grains of sand, She could let herself be carried with the wind being able to change from form into particles of sand, all in her colors, and in the wind she traveled his mind, seeing what he saw and thought.

If he should be torturing a minion or taking a virgin, she would see the notion form, take shape, become a wind taking sand and making a form of the minion or virgin and the grains, like her, became real in nature. She saw them suffering his torture, and learned she could fly through them, for they were all grains that were never solid, always changing. Inside the shapes, she could know their thoughts and feel their pain. Allowing herself fully inside a young virgin maid, she could take over her form and actions, and see through her eyes. She saw her father, vile and smiling, as he defiled the girl, and the girl existed in true form, Elsa able to be her in the mind of Lucifer's desert forms.

Before ever meeting her father, she knew his thoughts and actions, and knew he was evil for he knew right from wrong, good and bad.

Many times she would be seeing through his eyes, or be one he was defiling, but would return to grains of sand. That was when he changed his mind. There was nothing in the desert except what he thought, and it was a shifting, insane universe that made no sense. She lived in madness, and knew it was that. Lucifer understood he was insane.

On the day Gloria made her declaration, he traveled to his abaddon, into his thoughts. His form was only a manifestation of his true form which was a spirit having no physical substance. When all was made, the Thought, the Creator, wished to interact and touch things His mind created, and He thought of having form just as a tree or a leaf blowing in the wind. Using only the power of thought, His form took substance that looked to be a tree or a leaf, and it could touch things and be touched. That was the power of Thought, and all things were made from the Thought, nothing more.

It was not a host. It did not hold the spirit within, it was the spirit wishing to have form and be physical when desired. The form was a manifestation of the nature of the spirit. Male, female, smart, whimsical, young, old, funny or quiet, the form was the way Angels understood each other best. Form was the painting, the impression of the spirit within, but never fully physical as it was a projection, not matter.

Having no true physical nature, it was why Angels could "Will" to anyplace by thinking they wanted to be there. Without a physical body to travel in, they would think of the place they wished to be, and the wish to be there was all that was needed. Their form, pure projection, traveled with their Will, allowing them to go anyplace by wishing to be there.

When Gloria was young, she asked her father about the Blade. It struck the form just as his scythe struck wheat to cut it down. If Angels had no physical substance, how could the Blade strike one, such as Lucifer, and do harm. The Blade would cast him back to the place before he came to be. Nothingness. How could the Blade do anything at all to him? Michael thought it a wise question for one so young, yet an important one knowing what had happened to his wife, Ethereal, Gloria's mother.

"Like we take form, the power of our thoughts, our spirit, is one with the Creator. It comes from Him. That is the most powerful thing there will ever be. When I first held this Blade, it was nothing more than my scythe. It was my Knowing there must be a way to stop your uncle that changed it to the Blade. The Blade comes and goes. So, Gloria, when is the Blade seen?"

Holding the little mock Blade she made from a tree branch, she thought about it. She had never seen it fire but knew his Blade did when her father faced the hasataan.

"When my uncle is most evil and wants to harm us."

"That is so, and your Blade is not like the Blade of Divinity. It is wood and has substance. The Blade is not a thing. It is my Will to stop my brother. When threatening me, or you, or any Angel, my Will takes a form to let him know I will stop him, and it is my Will that powers the Blade. Actually, it is the Will of the Creator. He allows me to do what He can do. Send a spirit to nothingness, where it came from. The Blade is not just my wrath, it is the Wrath of God. It is His power, given to me to use with my discernment. That is why it only appears when there is a threat."

With granite crumbling and falling, Lucifer worried not for his form as it was not physical and could not be harmed. What he feared was what the nature of the Blade of Divinity held. The Will of Divinity to cast him to nothingness. It could not strike what could not be found, and at that moment, knowing a power was given to Gloria that was mightier than ever known, he Willed

Angel

himself into his own mind. A place he could only find. There, he was safe from the Will of the Guardian, Gloria.

The thunder she sent to abaddon was a warning that a new day had arrived. With her new Blade, she proclaimed she would be more than her father was, and mightier than anything had ever been. She could do more than strike him away, she could strike any doing harm or his work. That was the power of Creation, as the Creator could Will anything back to nothing, including Children and Angels. It was a new day, and he knew there was a new line and he had crossed it since he became hasataan. She would strike when she could find him, and that was why he had made abaddon in his mind. It was pure thought, and only Elsa knew how to go there.

That was troubling. He now had a second one to worry about, Elsa. She would strike him down, and being much the same as him, would befriend Gloria and together they had the power to destroy him, and the way to find him. It was why he had given Elsa the promise and hope of love with Michael, his brother. Her need for love was greater than his destruction. That could be done at a time of her choosing, a time when she and Gloria were aligned and understood each other. They both wished him to be no more.

Scroll Twelve

Having no understanding of things not embedded in her by Lucifer, her creator, her father, her nightmare, Elsa wandered Earth and knew little of Angels or their ways. Knowing only her father was once a First Angel of Heaven, the third Angel ever to be, he had fallen from what he referred to, with contempt, as Grace. Asking him questions was not her way, yet she was curious in her task of corrupting any with Grace, what Grace was, and why he despised it so. Just the question had him seething, but he understood it was a state of being she should know of.

"All that means is any being, child of Earth or Angel of Heaven, has the love of the one called Creator. That they are doing what he wishes, so he's not pissed at them. Me, I was the first to fall from Grace, and you, you hot snatch, have never been in any state of Grace. Not even mine."

Going no deeper, she understood him bitter as he had forsaken Grace for the one he called his Sweetness, some little child Angel. Knowing little of her, she only knew she was blonde, indescribably beautiful, and was now nearing being a woman in nature as she had no true age. At one time, Lucifer had gone off about how Gloria was his only desire as she was the Holiest of all Angels, but wouldn't be once defiled by the serpent,. Thinking of all her father had said, he wished for the most beautiful, holiest and most Divine Angel in all creation. It made sense to her that he would want only what he could never have to raise his standing to be beyond even God, yet to fail. Wanting what he could never have was a way to continue his need to be discontent in all things. It also explained why he had created her to be the same as Gloria in many ways.

Wanting to be God to all humans and Angels, he understood that all things were created by the Will of the Creator. Willful,

Lucifer knew he too could bring a soul into existence by sheer Will. It would give him equal status with the Creator, and all thought only the Creator could make a soul, or life. He decided to only create one such soul as he had no wish to be Father to more than one. That one would be of his nature, and the one who stood next to him, and if struck down by the Blade, would be the one next to be the evil he had created.

She was what else there was. Elsa. Made to be much like Gloria, but as he had longed for Gloria to be.

Where Gloria was good, he made her to do evil. Gloria was afraid, she was without fear of any except her father. Gloria was a virgin; she placed no value on sex. Gloria was a supreme warrior, she was a temptress, a seducer, one who could win any battle from a look, a nod, just letting herself be seen.

When created, she first had one thought and purpose, and that was to have sex with her father. To take his serpent and love it as the duty of being his daughter. When they first met, she told him she existed only to take his serpent and love him. Telling her she would learn from him what not having love from a father did to him, he had no love for her, and he would never let her love another just as his Father would not let him love Gloria. Telling her more, she was to take all who were loved by the Creator and seduce them. Defile them and have them fall from Grace. That was her only purpose. To take goodness from all who had it and make their souls his. Just as he was a beautiful Angel, she was a beautiful demon.

Laughing at the outcome, Lucifer had made her as planned, but did too good of a job. He had given her the need to be loved, and the ability to give true love to another. He planned it to be that only he would have her love, but that was not what happened. She despised him since created, and the need for love from one she admired grew stronger and made her wish to destroy her father.

In that, she and Gloria were equal. They each existed to destroy Lucifer.

Being made with the intelligence of Lucifer, she knew that until there was a way to cast him to nothingness, she must do his bidding. If not, she would never be able to destroy him. He would cast her away if she did not do all she was created to do, and be. It took time to understand the nature of his evil, and at first she thought nothing of taking souls in his honor. Using her seductive qualities, none could resist her. She was the alpha and omega for any she chose to take. Their beginning and their end. She was all that mattered to them once she looked at them. They were damned. Lost. Looking into her eyes, they began to shake in spasms of desire, lust, longing, craving, and they no longer valued anything except her. They would fall and die from an orgasm so intense it burst all the arteries in their hearts and brains. Their souls would rise, still reaching out to touch her. They never did. She would wave her hand and they were cast to abaddon.

Growing wiser, she learned that there was good and bad. Those holy, and those evil. She thought of what she did with her nature of taking souls and thought it wrong to do. That was also something Lucifer had not expected. With her own Will, being Free Will, she used her own mind. When tasked with taking a holy man or one revered for goodness, she had the power to see their true nature, their spirit. She would pass by ones true, and took endless ones who used the actions of being holy or righteous for power or to have women, but knew that whether or not she took them, they would not ever ascend to Heaven. She took only those destined to abaddon. More, she thought it good as Earth needed less such evil ones, and she dispatched them sooner, meaning they would have less chance to hurt others.

Lucifer's daughter appeared to do the work of the hasataan, but she knew she was not a demon.

Nor was she an Angel.

She was unique. Not Angel, demon or child of Earth, she was alone. The only one else. Elsa.

Apart from both Angel and Children of Earth, Elsa knew her father had created her to be a temptress, understanding that all in existence including Children, plants, animals, demons, minions, and also Angels were attracted to things beautiful. It was the way of things. The One who created her father had let all Angels know how He was once a thought in Nothingness and longed to be loved and according to her father, adored. Having created all things, He wished them to be pleasing to look at or touch for He had been alone through all eternity. When making Angels, each was beautiful to each other. They were made in the Mind of the Creator, making sense to her that what was attractive to him to view or know would create attraction from each of them to each other. Knowing her father was a First Angel, he was one of the most beautiful and she had seen him as Angel, and as the hasataan.

Angels were the highest level of beauty. Even the Children, Adam and Eve, were made beautiful and would have remained that way except for her father corrupting them. Falling from Grace, leaving Heaven, never allowed back as the ArchAngel Michael stood guard to protect his daughter, her father was filled with something beyond ire or anger. He had created hate. His hate was so powerful that he wished to be something new that would defy the nature of all Creation. He wished his own universe and his own order where none holy may enter.

Except for Gloria.

Falling from Heaven took an eternity to reach rock bottom where there was nothing more as the Creator had not yet thought of a place beyond rock bottom although it was there. Lucifer had time to seethe and think of how to be everything an Angel was not. Knowing Angels to be beautiful to behold, he wished to be repulsive to any Angel when he chose. Once in the hell of abaddon, he let his hatred shape his form. Having no beauty inside him, what formed was the hasataan. Hideous, foul, terrifying and putrid in all ways, he grew large and towered over the forms of the fallen Angels. Ten times taller than his Angel form, he was a giant that all could see when there was light, and all feared in light or darkness.

Growing before the eyes of his brother, Michael, sent to help the fallen, the hasataan was like nothing that any could ever imagine before that day. Only the insanity of her father could be so vile and deformed. As he grew ten times his size, large horns grew from his temples and they were curved and thick at the base where they grew from his head, ending in sharp points that could spear and impale not only the forms of the fallen Angels, but their souls. Knowing the nature of Angelic beings, he knew the form was just an illusion shaping the spirit of the Angels and his horns cut through their existences.

Hissing and growling, his teeth were likewise sharp and could bite the souls as he ate them. His eyes were pits of fire, flames rising from them, and the fire could be sent like beams to vanquish any who opposed him. The fire in his eyes could burn the soul from a form, casting to nothingness. His muscles were massive and had might to use a weapon that formed in his right hand. A trident having three long spears at one end which could strike through forms and impale them on the spikes, him holding the speared Angels to his mouth, eating their souls, growing stronger with each soul he took. His feet became hoofs, hard nails that could crush any in his path, and he became fully dark red with scales from the burning of his own flesh from the flames pouring from his eyes.

Behind him was a tail, and it was long and powerful with barbs on the end, and it too could sweep forms away or gather them on its barbs where it would swing around to put the one defying him in front of him where he would laugh, then in one movement put their entire form and soul into his mouth and feast on them. His entire form had transformed into a soul eater, and even his stare with its flames shooting at any he saw ended their existence.

Cowering from the hasataan, all except Michael feared him. It was when hasataan, still having the insane mind of Lucifer looked for Gloria and Ethereal in the thousands of fallen, realized he had fell for nothing. Ethereal was there, but had left Gloria behind in Heaven. The object of his transformation, the one he lusted for, was not there. Ethereal had deceived him. That sent a wave of shock through the gigantic cavern of black rock, all falling flat to the rock beneath them except for Ethereal. She alone was standing, looking at her brother, Lucifer, becoming the vile hasataan. She was far back in the cavern, and was fearful of getting her husband's attention as she knew Lucifer had transformed his madness to a new form and didn't want attention called to Michael.

Having never known anything of the sights that he saw, Michael was overwhelmed and confused. He saw Ethereal standing far away, but thought that she too had fallen. He had no way of knowing she fell only to save their daughter, so he thought only she had made a choice. To be with Lucifer, not him and Gloria.

Knowing Michael was confused, Lucifer hated his brother for being the perfect Angel. The First. One given the most wondrous Angel, Ethereal, while Lucifer was mated with none. Staring at Ethereal, then at Michael, Lucifer became beyond insane, beyond evil, beyond the destroyer he had made himself into. Looking at Ethereal, he thought the fire, his pitchfork, his tail or his rage were all insufficient to punish Ethereal for her deception. Boiling inside, feeling something he didn't understand, wanting to hurt Ethereal in a way all would remember and hurt his brother the most, he closed his eyes and the serpent grew from him.

Impossible to understand or imagine, the serpent grew from his groin, at first small, but it kept growing as it moved from him. Much like the snakes in the fields of Heaven, it was a writhing serpent that had slime and scales, two beads for eyes, and a mouth with sharp fangs and a forked tongue that flicked venom. Having a mind of its own, but commanded by Lucifer's Will, the serpent grew so long and large it reached to the back of the cavern where Ethereal stood. Floating above all cowered on the ground, it's eyes looked into hers as it reached her face, and its tongue flicked out and licked her mouth, then tore away her simple linen sheath. It circled around her, studying her form from every angle, and then moved back from her enough to look into her eyes again. They glowed red, and then its head lowered to her middle, circled behind her, and did the unknowable. It entered her, impaling her, and she screamed in such agony that her pain filled more than the cavern; it filled all existence.

Moving up inside her, it ate her hope, joy and heart as it impaled, then her head tilted back as its head exited from her mouth. Obeying Lucifer's Will, it lifted her up off the floor and began waving Ethereal above all those on the ground, showing them the power of the hasataan and his serpent, Ethereal hanging limp from the serpent impaled within her. Screams and wails of despair and fear filled the cavern, and the serpent moved to where Michael stood, frozen with shock, and put Ethereal fully before him as if standing there with him, but her head back, the serpent head out her mouth, its red eyes staring at him. It flicked its tongue, sending flicks of Ethereal's juices onto Michael's face. Hasataan watched with joy, his serpent doing his bidding better than he could have imagined. He laughed and taunted his brother.

"Ethereal is mine, brother. She is delicious. But know she is yours no more. She will only love and worship the serpent now, not you or Father. All women will crave the serpent now. The serpent will be only what any woman now worships."

Having the serpent take her from Michael, it put her at the hasataan's cloven hooves, laying there, as the serpent pulled from her and vanished back into his form. All had watched the horror, and the fallen Angels who at first wished to flee from the hell

Lucifer brought them to were now in fear of the serpent and hasataan's powers.

Michael heard the Creator say to offer all a way home, and his scythe changed to a Blade of pure light to guide the way. Wings like the birds that flew in Heaven formed behind him, a symbol of rising, flying away. They were not made of feathers, but of light that had the shape of feathers so all would know Wings were to rise up out of abaddon. Holding the Blade above his head, the light from his Wings and Blade filled the cavern with truth. For as far as could be seen, all the fallen Angels cowered in fear. He called to them, saying all were welcome back, for he was there to take them home.

"I am the way and the light. Follow me. Return to your Father and find Joy and peace."

As he began to ascend, not one fallen Angel came to follow. He rose slowly, giving all a chance, but they feared to even look as they knew the hasataan would eat their souls before they could reach Michael.

Michael ascended, alone, without Ethereal or any Angel. As he reached the entry to Heaven, he laid down his Blade, took large rocks and built an Arch at the entry. Taking his Blade, he used it to draw a line in the sand of the path. Standing there, changed, he would protect Gloria, and all in Heaven, from Lucifer or his minions forever. He would guard the Arch.

Declaring himself the ArchAngel, Michael shouted so powerfully that all in abaddon could hear him.

"Know this. I have drawn a line in the sand and stand guard at the entry to Heaven where there is now an Arch where I will be doom to any of abaddon who try to enter. No evil shall pass this Arch."

Elsa could see how beautiful Michael was, even more than before becoming the ArchAngel. A might grew inside of him that had an appeal much stronger than his form or appearance. He was her ideal of what attraction was. One who had more than beauty. He had power and was Holy. He protected Gloria.

She prayed for the first time. She asked the true Father to have Michael protect her.

Like Gloria, she needed protection from Lucifer. She was held by his chain, and she prayed that his mighty Blade could cut the serpent that choked her and bound her against her Will.

As she said her prayer, she Willed her burka away, and stood naked for Michael to see if he wished. She was small in height and in all ways. She was a wisp of a young woman, lovely as Ethereal or Gloria in form, but different. She had an allure that only one truly good could resist, knowing one such as Michael could see her the way she was, standing there. An innocent, born into a nightmare of evil, though she was not evil in any way. She feared her father, for the serpent around her neck was there to rip her soul from her form for Lucifer to eat. She was looking up, hoping Michael could see her pain, and the truth on her face. Her hair was dark brown as were her eyes. Her skin was silk and was glowing light. Her mouth was slightly open, showing a longing, a desire to kiss his mouth. Her cheekbones where high and softly blushing, and she was perfect in form. Every part of her was a curve leading to a place of mystery and pleasure. Her breasts were small, her legs long, her waist curving in then out to meet her hips. She only had eyelashes and hair on her head, no place else. Her hair blew in cascades that created shapes surrounding her body to hide parts, then reveal them.

Finishing her prayer, she rose from the ground, arms spread wide, head up, longing in her every part to be an offering of her form. That was all she knew how to do, but this time she felt her entire being offered to the ArchAngel. Her back arched, and she lay floating curved for him to see her true being inside her, her heart and her love, her desire for freedom and the love of a good man. She closed her eyes as she finished her prayer and imagined she was in Michael's arms, his new love, for he was the one her love had been made for — even though her father didn't realize that was what he had done.

Deep inside of Lucifer was shame. Guilt. Pain. He had destroyed Ethereal and taken what even he once loved. She was the mother of Gloria, and she had always accepted him even knowing he was sick.

Deep inside of Lucifer, Elsa knew that he made her to be for Michael. She was his repentance, though she knew he would never be forgiven.

Having forever meant she could be alone forever or be loved... if only one time and for a short while. It was all she wished for herself, knowing she had true love to offer in return. Her love, unlike her form, was unblemished. It was a true gift. Having her father command her to seek love from Michael was more than she had ever hoped for. She had been told by him to travel to sinners on Earth and hurt the Children of God to gain the attention of Gloria, having her descend, unguarded by Michael, to save the ones she would seduce.

It took a time long for Gloria to understand her Free Will allowed her to make such a decision. Learning the Creator would not interfere with the Free Will of any soul, Elsa too learned she had a choice. She could seduce those unholy looking at her in lust, or walk away. Following the wisdom of the Creator until then, Gloria, most holy of Angels, would not violate the Free Will of the Children she tempted, so never appeared. Lucifer's plan was that one day, she would, and that would be the day he impaled her as conquest. It was the most evil plan of all plans. It disgusted Elsa as it had no love, no art, no value except ego.

Considering a way to be free of her father's vile serpent around her neck, Elsa hid her nature when doing the work her father commanded of her. Covering herself in hijab and burka, she was fully covered from view. A dark veil covered the one opening for her eyes, allowing none to see her. Only the most despicable of those already destined for abaddon would be allowed to see her eyes, and that was all she needed to send them to a frenzy of death for her. Having no wish to do such to any who were good, she was kindred to Gloria in that manner as well. She fought evil, not empowered it, looking to Lucifer as if she were the most evil being except for him.

Being his temptress, the Children had moved from caves and being animals to form civilizations. Much of vile nature of Children stemmed from the influence of evil. Soon, in the desert which was the cradle of the new age of Children, empires rose, worshiping false gods, never the true Father. Influenced by Lucifer, he made deals for souls in exchange for powers to corrupt the new age of idol worship. Soon she was a false god to the foolish nobles, the pharaohs, the false prophets and priests and they were easy takes. Just a look, and they were doomed.

While in Thebes during the era when Egypt rose to become the cradle of a new world order, she met Gloria. It was a moment that was unexpected, and it was then she learned of how much her father lusted after Gloria, and how willing Gloria was to destroy his very existence. On that day, she knew that she would be aligned with Gloria and be her true friend.

Thinking back to her time being the seducer of the sinners of Egypt, she longed for any true affection or kindness. There was a first fallen Angel there harvesting women, and after a time watching over a queen who her father was grooming for her days ahead in abaddon, she turned to the vile harvester as he was the only one who understood she was truly alone, as was he. After the queen's soul was harvested by Lucifer with delight, free for a time, Elsa left the palace to be with the chosen harvester of women for Lucifer. In a moment of need, she made human love to the fallen one, Scorpio, and that was love for one other than her father. As they lay together in his modest home, Lucifer appeared. Having violated his command that Elsa love only him and no other, as a reminder he castrated Scorpio while floating over Elsa. Bleeding, in human form Scorpio was in pain and paying the price for a mistake she had made. Elsa ran to the market to find remedy for his pain after cauterizing the wound using fire. While searching for a serum, she encountered Gloria. It was a moment that she would never forget and she found comfort remembering that first meeting. Closing her mind to all other thoughts, she revisited that time.

Scroll Thirteen

Knowing Scorpio would feel pain being in human form, Elsa knew well it was her father's lesson to him to not fall again, although this time the fall was to Earth. He would feel the pain of love in his soul, and his form. Wishing to give him strength and heal his body, he was at rest given her command to sleep. When he woke he would suffer pain of body. Knowing him lost in sleep, she decided to venture to the market to find a remedy to disguise the pain. Looking at the white garb she had worn as a deception, it was now both red and turning brown having pressed it into Scorpio's wound, it was soaked in his lifeblood. Thinking it a reminder of the pain of love, she let it be. Waving her hand in front of her naked form, she became fully covered in a black burka, her face covered with a black face veil, her eyes were black pools of misery. No longer acting the timid maiden walking with a love not a love, Scorpio, she was the vengeance all would fear. Black as her father's soul, she would be innocent no longer. She would give her father no quarter; no room to dwell in her sadness as he had this day.

Walking through the market, all in her path parted to allow her to pass. She radiated her anger; her power had all cowering in fear. All knew that she was a demon from hell; none looking at her for fear she would unleash wrath upon them for the pleasure of causing them pain. She thought them feeble of mind, never able to see or know it was she who had been given pain beyond what any Child could know. With the wind blowing, her black garb was trailing behind her, her form fully revealed once more, brazen, a soul wounded and filled with pain. She was raging fire of beauty and wrath, all turning from her as she walked through the crowded streets.

Guided only by her pain, she stopped and looked at the carts and tents offering potions and useless tonics. She sought only that which would deaden pain of body, knowing only time would heal the wound yet an opium would mask any suffering. Even in the street she knew her father may deny even the juice of poppies as a reminder of his devastation. She cared not. She would face him if he appeared. Moving from her sense of where to go, she walked to an empty lane with nothing lining it, and no Children hiding from her there. She turned and looked down the lane and felt compelled to go there. Perhaps it was her father or a harbinger that called her. She cared not what waited there. If so, it would wait for her wherever she headed. Arms down and held behind her as if blown by a mighty wind, she slowly walked down the empty lane. As whenever her father appeared, the world stopped. All noise from the market went silent. Knowing she was the only one moving, the world was frozen, awaiting what was to come. All that existed was the wind, blowing her burka behind her, exposing her to what lay ahead, making her garb a banner of pain behind her. It was a moment no human could understand or see. Standing, she emptied her mind of all thoughts, resigned to wait for what was there for her alone.

Feeling a wind, it was change, coming from above. It was mighty and cleared all sand and dirt from the lane, sending it behind her. The lane ahead filled with a cloud from the sky above, rays of light parting the clouds to form a clearing most strange. This was not of her father. He hated light; he would have cast darkness around her. Hearing wind, engulfed in the light, she saw the one who was calling to her.

From the sky descended a vision more beautiful than she had ever seen. She was compelled to drop to her knees and cower before it. A force was lifting her, keeping her face looking to the sky. Seeing a blaze of light, the black cloth surrounding her changed to the purest white like the rays of light engulfing her, All fear and pain left her. For the first time since created she was filled with hope, with a sense of comfort and like love, something she had never known, Joy. She felt all suffering melt away, leaving her as if casting off a robe. Her arms raised above her, embracing the light and the beauty of the cloud which was blowing her pain away.

Feeling only warmth and peace, she watched as an Angel of God descended from above. Wearing only a translucent veil of the lightest gossamer, the Angel was made from the light, taking form with and from the clouds, the knee of one leg raised slightly, the other leg straight, pointing down to her descent, both arms bent upwards from her sides, a finger on one hand raised in a way to say she brought a message from the Father. Hair, light blonde, longer than could ever be imagined, was floating above her reaching to the Heaven she descended from, beautiful in movement taking shapes of glyphs that praised the Father. Her face was serene, kind, and Divine. Seeing the Angel filled Elsa with awe and comfort. The beauty given was beyond all she could imagine, and for the first time ever she wished she had been of Heaven, not of hell. Her mind emptied of all thoughts as the Angel grew near, the radiance filling her was all that existed in eternity.

Watching the Angel descend near to the ground, she marveled at the rainbow of colors in the clouds, the smell of Heaven's garden filling her with scents never known to her, feeling a warmth that embraced her and how the Angel was translucent as if a dream, yet a dream she could reach to and touch. The clouds surrounded them both, and she was lifted from the ground enough to have her eyes level with the Angel's. Her feet were several hands above where she stood as the Angel was tall when seen so close. The gossamer was only a wind that circled her, never actually touching her form, a body so flawless and perfect it was the reason for myths and legends, paintings and statues. Her face was the meaning of beauty, having features so ideal they had yet to even be imagined. Elsa knew only God could create such wonder, such perfection, and such comfort in her presence.

The Angel was beyond any dream. Beyond what Angels, demons or Children could imagine beauty could be. Elsa, versed in how form affected any, was as a beggar in the lane, asking for alms that would be words or thoughts of what was before her. The Angel was more than form, more than spirit, more than radiant, more than what could ever be. Her father had a profound effect on those seeing his form. The Angel was much more than a force. The power blowing her away to eternity yet keeping her there. It was a sensation that made her feel like a moth to a flame. Pure light, pulling her to that which could destroy her, though she knew that would not be. Facing the Angel, Elsa felt no bigger than a moth next to her. Knowing she was made to be small and innocent in form, the Angel was tall and was more than innocent. She was Holy. Majestic. She gave comfort yet was one who must be feared for she was radiating vengeance and power that was far beyond even the hasataan. She felt humbled, dwarfed in every manner, yet felt loved and safe. It confused her and this was no fallen First Angel. This was the true Angel. Magnificent in every way.

Her eyes were pools of blue that never remained the same shade, changing in swirls of every shade of blue. Her skin was not skin. It was translucent showing her very soul, it being more beautiful than her form, yet had the illusion of physical being. Her lips were soft and what the nature of lips were, not like lips at all. Her hair was blonde, yet not blonde at all. It was the idea of what blonde hair was. It was the wish to see blonde hair, the ideal of what most of Earth had not. Each strand was a thought, a wish, a notion calling her to have it encircle her to keep her safe. Ever moving, her hair was forming glyphs only Angels could read, saying, "Joy, I am Angel of God, I am here." Her form was not what Children knew. She was long and tall, like the most beautiful tree growing in the light of Divinity to seek the light of God. Her curves were like her hair. The idea of what perfection must be, what a form could be if Blessed. Her legs were long, and she was an idea, not a form. She was what any imagined beauty must be, but none capable of imagining what beauty was. The Angel was what all beauty would ever hope to be.

Elsa realized the Angel had descended with Wings raised straight up to the sky to fit in the narrow lane. Made from pure light that formed the shapes of feathers, they were the way feathers felt, not what feathers were. The Wings rose so high she couldn't see their ends as they reached beyond the cloud. It was her first time encountering a true Angel as she had only known the fallen, and they had no Glory, no such beauty, and no Majesty. They had left all Divinity in Heaven when they fell. She shuddered realizing Scorpio had given up such Majesty. She pondered how hasataan had compelled the others to give up such splendor, how any could choose to live in dark when they were once the stuff of dreams, loved and safe, never hiding or plotting revenge and pain. She understood all fallen were fools, pawns of evil, glad she was not of the fallen. For a moment she knew if she were created as Angel, she would be such comfort and Joy as the one she saw before her. Tears ran down her cheeks in sadness for even if she gave herself to the Father, begged His love, if He welcomed her to His home, she could never be such an Angel. She could take the form this very day, appear as one such, but she had no power to radiate comfort or serenity. It saddened her.

The Angel knew all she thought, all she felt, and her eyes told of her love for all. She saw the Angel close her eyes, gently, and her manner shared a hint of sorrow. Such a feeling touched Elsa with sadness that was profound. It was pure. A wind that blew her contentment in a new direction, not leaving, just feeling how Joy and sorrow sit together and how the balance could change. Looking to the ground below, the Angel shook her head, then returned her gaze to Elsa who grew frightened as the Angel had seen a site most sad. Holding her right hand up above her head, a Blade appeared in her hand, blinding as it was made of pure light. The Angel's left hand lifted to be in front of Elsa's face, one finger raised, assuring her, telling her to worry not. With that understanding, Elsa was lifted higher, just rising in the air with no feeling of being pulled, having no fear of falling. The Angel looked down and Elsa followed her gaze. The Angel descended, though only a short way, to the ground as the clouds parted and Elsa saw what had occurred below.

Holding the Blade with both hands above her right shoulder yet now out to her side, the Angel stood ready to strike, intent on the one before her. Elsa's father, Lucifer.

Filling with shock her father would appear to challenge the Angel, she realized her father was Angel once, thus knowing what power he challenged. Knowing he once faced the Blade the day abaddon was created, he faced it once more. He was bold and fearless, showing no caution. He stood with his arms crossed, waiting, showing no concern for the only power that could strike him down.

The two Angels stood facing each other. One pure light, one pure dark. She saw her father's face as never before. His eyes were gentle, his head moving slightly in a direction that followed his gaze as he looked at every part of the Angel. He was nodding in admiration, clearly showing lust and longing as he looked at all her form many times. The Angel floated motionless, ready to strike. The blaze of the Blade lit his face and Elsa saw him true for the first time ever as the light revealed only what was, not what he wanted all to see. He was beautiful. Though having no Majesty, no Divinity, he still had the perfection of an Angel from Creation, one of the first. With his beauty revealed by Divine light, he denied any such Knowing, wishing only there be visage most repulsive. The spirit inside flowed out, corrupting his perfect form, making it ugly and deformed but not to the Angel. He had a manner that fooled all as he could charm and deceive. He made no attempt at such illusion as he looked at the Angel. Knowing he had purpose, the Angel, clear, revealed she cared not of his intent. She spoke fully, with Voice, and was certain in manner but gentle in tone.

"Uncle, I will use this Blade."

Elsa's whole body shook as if she had been hit with the mightiest weapon ever known. She was astounded as she was witnessing Heaven versus hell. Lucifer facing the only object of his desire. The one he fell for, damning all who would ever be for eternity, only to have her, the Sweetness.

"Gloria, I am certain you will. You will have no use for it as I offer no threat. I will tell your mother how her beautiful girl has become a beautiful woman. There can be no other to equal you. I long only for you."

Not moving, still ready to strike, Gloria was certain in her manner, having no patience for such deceptions.

"That matters not to me. I have mother no longer. She is free to return home unless you have chained her as you only stop any with such sad hold."

Her father shook his head, slowly, his eyes continuing to covet her.

"She has always been free to ascend. None has never been gifted with her presence. She hides in shame. I assured her she has nothing to be ashamed of. If she wished to return, I could not stop her. You know that."

Gloria remained as if a statue, but the sword raised slightly, more menacing, brighter.

"Lie to yourself. Divinity knows only truth. Do not lie again, Uncle."

Laughing, Lucifer shrugged his shoulders and nodded.

"Hark, my Sweetness, you will hear truth. It was you I craved, taking your mother as I thought she would hold you tight as she fell. Ethereal is forever a disappointment to me as she hasn't given me what I want. You."

Gloria raised the Blade and turned to striking position. Elsa trembled at the sight. She now, for the first time, knew fear. It was horrific and she could only watch the two as they sparred.

"That matters not to me. That was folly. Even then, daughter of the Guardian, this Blade would have formed from me, not my father. I would have struck you down. This you know, and why you fell without me. Now, uncle, I have purpose. It is not for you.

Why are you here? I warns you. Leave."

Shrugging again, he gave a look most deceptive, a mockery of truth.

"A father is right to protect his daughter. My Elsa was out shopping, and you have appeared though not called. That worries me. The question is why are you here? You were not called."

Gloria raised the Blade fully above her, the tip pointing down to Lucifer's heart.

"Where I go is no concern of yours. You interfere with my intent. That is cause to strike. I have been kind and not done so yet, but know this, I speak true. You have crossed the line."

With her last word, Gloria drove the Blade of Divinity straight down to strike Lucifer. At the same moment, he was gone, vanished. Knowing he had interfered with her action, he had anticipated she would strike as she had promised and done.

Lucifer gone, the Blade vanished, and Gloria rose from the ground and Elsa was lowered. Meeting eye-to-eye, Gloria held out her arm, giving Elsa a parchment tied with a string. As Elsa took it, Gloria looked up, then with her arm raised, her form flew skyward, taking all clouds with her. Elsa gently reached the ground, standing with the parchment in her hand. Time had returned, and she heard the noises of the marketplace and people walking by. Looking up to the sky above, she stood staring, thinking of the glorious Angel and how powerful she was. Looking around her, she saw a large rock. She went to it, sat, still looking upwards, then all around to see if her father stood nearby, waiting. Both were gone.

Letting all that happened fill her, she looked at her burka. It was silk and most beautiful. She smiled at the gift, Knowing it was a sign to cast off the darkness of the day. She held the parchment in front of her, and feeling it was more than it appeared. Untieing the simple string, putting it in her pocket, she pulled the parchment open. Inside there was a simple bottle. A vial filled with liquid. Holding it up to see its contents, it was clear. Holding it in her hand, grasping it firmly, she read a message in the scroll.

"This will heal body. Only love heals pain."

Under the message it was signed, "Gloria."

Scroll Fourteen

Learning that Scorpio was not worthy of any love for he was as corrupt as her father, Elsa left him to the sad practice of harvest. Unlike her, he had been an Angel in Heaven, and was the first to follow Lucifer to abaddon. Wishing to gain favor, it had been Scorpio who offered to harvest the women of Earth to give Lucifer more souls, giving him ever greater power. He was a deceiver, the first of many fallen to rise to demon status, and had spent little time in abaddon past the first days after the fall.

While punishing Scorpio for showing affection of sorts to his daughter, Lucifer learned how powerful Gloria had become. Having the Blade of Divinity, he knew that if he encountered her, if he took no action to harm her or lie about such intent, the Blade would not fire and he would remain safe. Though a deceiver in all matters, he was smart enough to put the limitation of the Blade to his advantage in seeking to have encounters with Gloria. All he need do was to evade, avoid, or not think of sinful acts, but not hide the truth. The truth would always be that he wished to take her and that could cause the Blade to strike. A master of manipulation, he could encounter her and never respond to such a question, tell of his intent, and could use his Will to deny any such topic by thinking of another.

Being arrogant from his power over fallen Angels and Children of Earth, he decided to be party to actions he did not initiate, but would be there or the indirect cause of something that would call Gloria to interfere in some manner. His experience with acting with concern for Elsa when she encountered Gloria the first time was from his harming Scorpio, but not Gloria. The Creator and Michael had a line that protected Heaven and Angels, but not his minions or Children of Earth. His plan was to create such evil that Gloria, righteous from the loss of her mother, would eventually wish to protect others harmed by Lucifer, and she would descend to protect them. In such instances he could be present, and there would be a moment of distraction where he could seize her attention and sway her loyalty.

Knowing she wanted no harm to others, his intent was to reason with her. It would be as simple as saying that if she wished such harm to stop, for all evil to vanish, she could be the savior of all by being his intended mate. Once with him, he would find his Joy and have no need to attract attention by harming others. It would be a simple deal, and he was skilled at deal making. He would say join him, be his, and he would stop all sin. If she truly wished to save all from harm, it was a simple decision. Join him, save all. Repel him, he would hurt all in every way possible. It was despicable, repulsive, and he knew she would have no love for such an offer, yet it was a way to save all creation from his evil.

If she denied him, he would question why she didn't want to save all from damnation. He would ask her if her virgin pride meant more than the souls of all created. It would be a sacrifice, but wasn't she putting her own self above all others? He honored all deals, and would fulfill his part of the bargain.

His plan was to shame her. She was already the sole reason he fell from Heaven and created sin. She suffered that shame, and he would add to it as she could be the one to end it.

With such shaming, there was no threat and no harm to her, and the Blade would not stop him.

Elsa knew he learned from her encounter with Gloria that he could taunt, cajole, imply, and that was not cause for the Blade to strike. He tested the Blade with his last taunt and had escaped. Knowing where to draw his line, he would take actions that would attract Gloria's attention, and he was sending her away to keep her from warning Gloria what he was doing. She knew her father well, but had Knowing from the encounter with Gloria. Just as her father had a plan, so did Gloria. Her father would taunt, thinking he was the only one smart enough to use such a plan, but it would be just as possible for Gloria to taunt him and make him cross the line without his realizing it. It was to become a battle of Wills, and in the matter she knew Gloria would have the advantage for she was rational; Lucifer, insane. His arrogance would cause him to cross the line. She thought long of how going to Heaven to seek love from Michael could help Gloria. She was gifted with the immense knowledge of her father's ways and would give Gloria insight into the harm she was enduring, and that may be a way to encourage Gloria to know her advantage.

At first worried that Gloria would view her seeking love from Michael as crossing the line to hurt an Angel, she stopped her worry. She could only harm Michael if she had such intent. She didn't. She realized that it was Michael who could best understand what being the daughter of Lucifer meant. It was never her Will to be his daughter, and because she had been forced to do his bidding, it was the serpent around her neck that kept her slave to his perversion. If any could remove the serpent from her, it would be Michael. He was good, not evil, and he had love for Gloria and all that existed. She existed, and she would seek his love. It would be true love, not harm or deception.

Commanded to give love to Michael, Gloria would know her love to be true. She would be honest that it was her father's bidding, she would leave him at some point, but that she wished to be loved, and to love one who could accept her and that was true beyond all else. It was what all had, few understanding the gift the true Creator had given. For her it was the curse of being not of the Creator, not of one Holy, the one who was without love.

Deep within her was a longing to know why Gloria was the most Holy, the most beautiful in all Creation, and why her vile father would give even her to have the Sweetness. Such attraction was a mystery to her, though she had always been *She Who Must Be Desired, She Who All Craved*. She was the meaning of lust and desire to all, yet they were not praises in her mind. They were lures to steal souls, nothing more. Each time someone began to call her "She," it was her wish to hear them say "She Who Must Be Loved." That had never happened. Showing ire at being called the one who must be desired, worshiped, wanted, craved, obeyed, soon the Children of Earth who spoke of her stopped using the epitaphs, learning the only way to refer to her was, "She."

Wandering through the busy alleys of Thebes, in the middle of the vast desert where a caravan was camped, in a church or an entombing chamber, though covered so fully no part of her could be seen, just her presence had all fallen to the ground before her, uttering "She." Like a leper, in a crowded place all people parted to give way, turning from her as she passed. It was the way it had been and would be, and she was ever alone.

None cowering were of interest to her as reaper of souls. Her visage worked to identify fools, and they were the only ones standing when all else fell with respect for her power. Those standing were the ones she would take. Long past any ritual, she would walk up to them, lower her veil and look into their eyes. That was all. She would walk away to the next one standing as the one seeing her eyes fell in spasms of orgasm, their hearts exploding and veins in their heads bursting. There was no need to be sure. They were already in abaddon. The ones cowering would look up, see the one thrashing in a sick mix of delight and death, and knew they lived by turning away from She, for she was the hasataan sent to harvest the wicked. Turning away meant they were not wicked and had no attraction to her offering.

Furthering her knowledge of the Children, she came to understand that those who were good, not following in her father's ways, cowering when she came near, knowing her to be the devil on Earth, had a pattern. The ones who stood and sought themselves to be above the power of the hasataan were most often the ones having wealth or power. Such advantages were not enough for fools spending their existence wanting such meaningless things. They wanted to be above all else, above even Lucifer. That is why she thought them fools, worthy of her glance.

Learning the ones kneeling, head to the ground, looked as if in prayer at a mosque or at prayer hour. They said no prayer to her or her father. They simply wish to never see evil or know it. Like the ones foolish enough to stand before her, the ones cowering were the poor, the disheartened, the lost, the lonely, the ones starving. They were humble and asked nothing of her other than to pass them by. Although she could not stop and talk to the ones kneeling in fear, she understood them to be the meek, the ones who would enter Heaven, not abaddon. She wished she could be that simple and free. To live a simple life then ascend for not bowing to evil, ever fearing it. Not all on the ground were holy. Many were thieves and fornicators, liars, and beggars. Seeing such as ways to survive, nothing more, she knew good from evil. If they suffered any sin, it was the need to eat. They were poor.

Walking down a street one day, she saw the ones cowering before her, and Willed her burka pockets to be filled with abundance of gold satars. As she passed by the ones with their heads to the ground, she dropped a handful of the gold discs before each one, an amount that would last them a lifetime. Soon, she became a legend that the humble would be gifted by She, the arrogant and mighty cast down. None were foolish enough to beg or rise up to see if they could get her attention for more gold. One had tried that first day and she looked at him, and he went into spasms without orgasm, suffering without any gift of her countenance. All others heard the story and knew that a gift was from not asking, respecting her wish to be hidden behind her veils.

Her gifting the humble soon gave her a devoted following who had been blessed with her gift, not death. Statues of "She" began adorning homes and shops, and there were special prayers to her after ones to Allah. She was not a god, not holy, but thanked for her passing by, and by understanding they had little other than fear. All knew she was of hasataan, a reaper of souls, but they could give thanks she took only the "little hasataans" that made them slaves or paupers. Never giving satars for respect, she gave them for a special purpose. Knowing they would one day ascend to Heaven, it was her hope that Gloria and Michael would be told of the veiled hasataan, She, and how giving and fair she was to the ones who had faith.

She no longer met with Scorpio. At first, she knew it would be a risk as her father would punish him more for any affection shown, but soon she realized that he was as evil as her father. He was one who delighted in the harvest, not hate it as she did. He was a deceiver and had never loved her or wished to show her love. Having her was only a way to raise his status as demon, nothing more. She knew he would not be allowed such pride. Her father was not finished with Scorpio and would do more to put him in place, but still would have him as harvester of women. He was good at it, and it was a sad, sick existence so a way to make Scorpio suffer more each day. He had women but loved none. None loved him. He was a slave harvesting grain night and day, but never having bread to nourish him. He was a starving demon, like her. She had no choice as she was made by Lucifer. Scorpio chose to be in his service. She hadn't.

With her order to find Michael and seduce him, Elsa knew her father would not use her to get Gloria to Earth. He did know Gloria had appeared to give comfort to one hurt by her father, it was Scorpio that he would use to attract Gloria to descend to the streets of Thebes.

That was for Scorpio to endure, and her decision was to go to Michael in Heaven, and to have Gloria as a friend who would hear her speak true. The way to be free of the chain placed on her by her father was to reveal his plan to Gloria and Michael, revealing her wish was only to find love with him.

Scroll Fifteen

Walking past his small grotto, Michael carried a basket Gloria had woven from reeds made for gathering fruit. Passing many groves of fruit most ripe and ready for harvest, he knew of a grove that bore strange fruit that was seldom picked and was ripe. So few passed on the road he thought it a good destination and there he would find some for his table. Although Gloria was away and there were many gatherings about, he was content picking fruit, walking alone in prayer, giving himself to all truth. Looking at the road ahead he knew the road went on forever, yet had an end. In teaching Gloria, he loved looking at the ordinary things around them, thinking of them as the Father truly made them, showing how all things are a mystery and even if the mystery is believed solved, the answer would become a mystery.

Many times, Gloria would listen to him and though she fully understood enigma, waiting for him to present such quandaries, she would stand with her face tilted, looking at him, and he would see the light in her eyes shine with the way she embraced the endless spirals of contemplation. He smiled as he recalled a recent walk with her when they saw an Apple that had dropped from a branch onto the road. He held out his arms, and they stood looking at the apple there before them.

"Daughter, on this road, we find we are not the only ones who travel it. What of this apple? Did it wish to be here? Was it tired of being an apple on a tree and decided to be a traveler? Did it wish us to find it? What was it yesterday and what will it be tomorrow? An apple can be many things. It is a surprise, a joy to see, a reminder that we are all apples on our road. As you stand here, what does it inspire in you?"

Putting her hand on her chin, thinking as she looked at the apple, her eyes raised with awareness, she looked at him, nodded, bent down, took the apple from the road, stood up, facing him and took a bite. She offered him a bite, saying, "It inspires me to take a bite. Father. It's an apple. You eat them."

Thinking of that moment on his walk, he thought of the mystery of how she could see the apple for what it was, yet he wished it to be more. He had long thought he was teaching Gloria, but now it seemed she was the one teaching him. Knowing the apple could be an infinite number of things, he had been rescued from getting lost in what anything could be by observing her acting on what anything was most likely to be. Standing in the road looking at the apple he could have questioned its meaning for endless days. Never reaching an answer, if he finally decided on the obvious, that it was a nice treat, it would have rotted away. Gloria showed that accepting it was a ripe apple to be eaten, she enjoyed it for what it was. It was an apple, a gift, it was its own answer.

After they both enjoyed the fruit, then laughing about how crisp and juicy some mysteries were, he teased her about her philosophy, asking her of the mystery of how the apple got there.

"True, daughter. It was fine fruit, but do you ever wonder how the apple came to be? Before it fell to the road, before it was on the branch, before it grew, before the tree? Where did it come from? What is an apple?"

Again, she stopped and looked at him. She taught him a lesson long forgotten, and it was the first lesson any must learn.

"Oh, father. An apple is a gift from God. He created the ground, the water, the seed, the apple, the road, and us to eat it. All things have the same answer. It's the first thing you taught me."

Seeing a valley off the side of the road, he stopped and recalled the day when he shared such wisdom with Gloria. Abaddon had not yet been created. The fall, the Garden, sin. All that was God's gift was not yet used to hurt Him many times. The apple in the road may be a temptation to sin, as was so in the Garden. Evil and sin had put doubt in all things. Wishing all others to suffer, those in hell learned that by poisoning Joy, looking at the apple as a gift was no more. He once spoke to his brother Lucifer and had no doubt of his words or actions. That changed. Lucifer planted the seeds of doubt in all things. Many new words were needed to speak of things never known before Lucifer. He thought of the word he wished most to not hear. Trust. Children on earth had obscenities for evil acts. Dirty words. Things soiled and ruined. So many beautiful things were soiled by sin. Being unable to trust was obscene to him. Children thought only fools trusted anyone. Evil had spoiled even God and love for them. It had made all in Heaven wonder if the ones they knew and loved may be the next Lucifer. It had happened, so it could happen again. It was unfair to think all loved were the next Lucifer. That was understood. The seed of doubt planted by his own brother required a new word. He and Gloria had met with Father after Lucifer and Ethereal fell from Grace, asking how they could trust even those closest to them. He taught them a new word. Faith. In Him, and all ahead. They both questioned faith. It would mean believing without knowledge or being sure trust was deserved. That was where Gloria learned to pick up the apple and trust in it. Father had used an apple to explain faith. He said while there may be one apple, at some moment, other than what it seemed, without trust all would starve. He left it at that. Faith was the only weapon against evil and sin. It applied to all souls and all things. Gloria had shown him how important it was to have faith and to trust in their own judgment. He was struggling with trust and was sad, having little Joy. Gloria trusted. Most important she trusted her instincts. She smiled and was Joyous. She had lost her mother, saw his hurt, yet she had faith in love, him, and the Father.

It was on the road, the one where he had found his faith and trusted in God, he saw a small form ahead. A woman, small in frame, gentle in manner, beautiful in visage and form, standing reaching up to take an apple from a tree branch. She was wearing a flowing burka of white silk, her hair was dark brown, and she aroused a feeling in him he had long forgotten. He found her attractive, and he thought only to go to her, help her, not who she was. Her visage was calling him, drawing him to her. He knew all in Heaven yet did not know her. She was a mystery. He recalled the apple and how Gloria took it and ate. Without questioning his thought, seeing her there, stretching her slim form up to the branch, he saw an apple. He wanted a bite.

He felt elation as he went to her, stood next to her, and reached the apple she was looking to, took it, and handed it to her.

Taking it with both hands, she took a bite, appearing very hungry, closing her eyes as she tasted it, then opened her eyes and they were staring up into his. The apple in both her hands, held before her mouth, looked large and moist, showing her bite in it with its juice running down its red skin. Her eyes kept sight to his. Swallowing the first bite she licked her lips, then spoke to him in a voice sweet as the apple.

"Thank you, so much. I was very hungry. You saved me…"

She held the apple up to his mouth, wishing to share it with him. Although he could easily reach for another apple, hers was the only one he wished. He leaned over and took a bite from where her teeth had bit while she held it for him. It had been long since any food or simple thing had given him joy, but the bite was delicious. It was as if having his first bite of any fruit, ever. She smiled as she nodded to him.

"Please sit with me. I have traveled far, and this tree offers shade. It offers us company."

She held the apple as she sat on the ground, her white linen showing the graceful shapes of her pleasing form. He was compelled to sit close to her, facing her, wishing to see her beauty. She let him study her. Moving slightly to show him her face different ways, knowing he hoped she would do so, she turned to

134   Angel

face him, then took another bite, sighed with the pleasure of it then spoke to him, gently.

"It seems I am not the only one hungry. Nor am I the only one traveling this lonesome road. I am most glad you found me. I must tell you, I am but a seeker, and I was searching only for you."

Michael was still entranced, but her words gave him surprise. He realized she was truly a mystery on the road. He sought words, and they came.

"I can only speak true. I am taken. I am entranced and that means much. I saw you reaching and all that mattered was helping you. Then, knowing you. Now, being with you, by your side. Those are things I can not explain. I know all here, but not you. Yet you say you were searching for me, so you know me. Are you real? This seems but dreaming."

She reached out with one hand, the other still holding the apple, then gently rubbed his arm. She nodded gently, again, and kept her gaze fixed on him.

"A dream. Real. Does such matter? They are the same as they are what we know. I am a dream and a waking. You have been a lonely traveler, and here you are, in my oasis. Enjoy it. Existence has become a desert. For you. For me. What do any wandering the desert seek? An oasis. Shade. Water. Comfort. Rest. Do you realize that you have been in a desert? That you have been searching?"

All she said was true. Michael had not wished to accept that since Ethereal fell, he was in a barren land even with the love of Father and his daughter. The oasis she spoke of was the special place where two joined in love and were one. He knew he was under a spell, yet it was comforting. She offered no harm, only kindness. He did wish to know of her, how she knew of him, and he asked her. She leaned back, her breasts small mounds rising in the white linen, her face an invitation and destination. So little, yet so much inside. She spoke with longing and wishing him to be knowing of all she was.

"My journey to you was long, and at last I have found my way. I am reaching up, as I hunger for good, like this apple. I will speak true, and I ask only you listen. I escaped from a prison, and only here am I safe. I am not of Heaven. I am not of Earth. I am not of abaddon. I am not Angel, Child, or devil. I am one with no home. Never born, created, like Adam. Not of the Father. Created, without mother, from seed of Lucifer, your brother. Created as you see me, never infant, never child, but truly just girl who is woman. I rose from his seed soaking the sand in a desert beyond all eternity. I have his powers but want them not. Unlike him or any of hell, I alone have love. My father has forbidden my love to any but him. He has a hold on me that I cannot break, but I need to be loved, and give love. I have known of you always, since made. That only you have domain over your brother. I have dreamt of you, saving me from him. That dream is all I am. Know this. You saw me as a dream this day as you have forever been my dream. Being here with you can only be a dream. In Heaven. With one who loves, not hates. One who can see the tender love in me. I know my beauty is sweeter than this apple, but know my beauty is truly the love inside of me. That is the dream you feel. Suffering the wrath of my father, I was saved by the Grace of your sweet daughter, Gloria. Graced with Vision of her Divinity, I gained strength to escape and find you. I know the way into Heaven as my father knows this land and has told me of it. That was why I was able to enter. Not a demon of hell, nothing forbids me to enter. That is how I arrived this day. Michael, I am Elsa, and I seek your love."

Scroll Sixteen

Reclined on the grass in the shade of the grove, Michael knew if he was in the presence of any evil, even if only a desire, the Blade of Divinity would be blazing in his right hand. It could not be deceived even if Angels could be. There was an order in Creation, impossible to understand by any but the Father. The Blade was made from the fabric of all things, like life itself. It knew nothing of intent, had no judgment, no Free Will, and heard no stories. It appeared only when the force of existence was challenged. It was the power of Creation. When all was made, God looked at his work and thought it good. When evil appeared, God saw it was not good, but was part of what He created. Michael, having drawn a line in the sand saying Heaven was where no evil may enter, the Blade appeared to guard His Angels and Heaven as evil existed only to destroy His work. Using the source of Creation, He forged the Blade to use the power of the first day if the line to Heaven, to all good there, was crossed.

Having faith in Creation, his Father, and the certainty of the Blade, he accepted that Elsa was as she said. She was the creation of Lucifer, handed a cruel existence, and had love in her which prevailed over Lucifer's wishes for her. He could not be certain of all things, but to know the truth he decided to allow it to be revealed, not run from it. In doing so, he found himself laying on the ground in front of one created to do evil, saying she wished love to break the chain that bound her to Lucifer. Michael had lost his wife, Ethereal, to Lucifer's chain. He wished to free Elsa and love was the only way.

Elsa was made to seduce any. Michael fully understood for she told him she was so. Her very being was enticement, attraction, desire, lure. Just as the leaf in the tree branch above him could only be a leaf, Elsa could only be temptation and desire. Seeing her, his every impulse, thought, wish, was to grab her, rip away her burka and be inside her. Having never experienced lust before, it shocked him as it was so complete and had such power. Provoking such lust, he asked if she could she not do such. He needed it not to want her. She leaned over him, letting him feel her breath, and whispered in his ear.

"No. I am desire."

She moved her head where her face was over his, a breath away, her eyes over his, her mouth over his, staying there. He realized that he was rubbing her body, and he was pulling her white sheath away, off her. As the white silk slid away, her eyes showed excitement and her breathing deepened. He put his hands on her, and her skin was smoother than the silk. It was telling his hands where to go. They moved over hills and valleys, long roads, sacred places, his hands welcome everywhere he reached, hearing her sigh as he touched her over and over in all places. He felt wetness from her open mouth drip into his, tasting her. She put her small hands on each side of his face, rubbing his cheeks, his temples. Her thumbs pressed into his cheeks, gently coaxing his mouth to open. Moving her head up to where he could see her mouth, it was open. She closed it for a moment, then her lips formed a circle, a stream of her spit flowing down into his mouth. Just seeing the stream coming from her was telling him she wished to be in him, and he wanted her to be. Opening her mouth once his was full, her tongue circled her lips, and she told him to swallow and know the spit was her. As he drank it, she would be in him, become a part of him. His blood, his every part, his thoughts would now have her in them. He swallowed and he could feel all she said. She was true. She was in him. Then she asked him to fill his mouth so he could be in her the same way. He closed his mouth and he found it filling with his own spit. When full, he opened it, and she put her mouth over his and sucked all his spit up into her mouth, then quickly raising her head, tilted it back, opened her mouth and swallowed all he had gathered for her. He could see the slight bulge in her throat as she took all in one swallow. Throwing her head back down, she stopped to look into his eyes, then her tongue went into his mouth and he found he was sucking it, trying to pull all of her into him. Her lips were pressed fully against his, and she turned her head slightly allowing full contact between them. Her body was writhing as he was still holding her, and she was using her legs to part his robe, letting it fall to his sides. Skin against skin, he felt her everywhere. He was fully erect, and she had been rubbing herself on him there, softly up and down, making him harder and harder, her other lips kissing him there and they were wet as her mouth. As naturally as looking into her eyes, he found he was inside of her. She had moved herself to where there was no other place he could be. All of him was inside her and she moved her head back, looking at him, her mouth open slightly, nodding in rhythm with her hips. Her knees moved forward on each side of him, and kneeling so, she sat up, making herself a straight line above him. Moving up and down, hips rocking forward and back at the same time, putting both arms out to her sides, needing only him inside. He saw her fully for the first time, saw all of her body ripple in waves as she moved, her breasts moving only from breathing, her stomach moving in and out, then her head falling back, her throat and entire form now one perfect line up from him. Arms straight out to her sides, she was the most beautiful thing he had ever seen. He saw her inside and out and seeing her body and spirit in such passion was perfect beauty. She had given all she was to him. It was beyond anything he had ever known.

It was the moment when he saw her total being, that she was his, that they were one, now in each other, he completed the union in an explosion of all he was, now inside her. Her head flew forward, her stomach was a hollow cave sucking his gift into her, her hands landed on his chest, she looked at him, panting, her mouth open, bottom lip pushed out. Her tongue over her bottom teeth, her body was in spasms, twitching, each spasm causing her eyes to roll. With one final seize that squeezed all juice from him, she collapsed onto him, gasping for air.

Still twitching, panting, she lay on top of him in total peace, total surrender. Her arms slowly worked their way to his sides, rubbing him, then they moved to where she put her hands on his cheeks, looked up from his chest, moved up as she slid off his cock, being so small she worked at moving up to where her face was finally over his. Holding his cheeks tight, she looked at him with intense longing, then kissed him, tenderly and with love. Letting herself slide back down a short way, she laid her head on the top of his chest. She was rubbing his hair, his face, his shoulders. Her legs were rubbing him, and he found she had wrapped herself around him and it was where she wanted to be.

As they lay embraced with utter contentment, they both jumped at the shock of hearing something most unexpected.

"Daddy!"

Head raising up, looking to Gloria, she looked back at Michael, showing eyebrows raised wondering what he wanted her to do. He lifted his head up, seeing Gloria standing on the edge of the road near them. Both of her hands were up on each side, her body showing both shock and a question of what he was possibly thinking. She stood there, stunned, waiting for any reply.

Having no shame as he felt they had not done any wrong, he knew instantly that unprepared, Gloria didn't know what had happened, or what to think. Being what she was, he also knew as Guardian, her nature was to protect him as he may have been in peril even if he didn't know it. He called out to her.

"Gloria, I am safe. Please, I ask you to come sit here. I know this is most unexpected. Come, let me calm any worries."

He looked at Elsa, and she nodded, giving him a simple smile of understanding, slid off to his side and sat on the ground with her knees up and her hands wrapped around them. Michael sat up, pulled at his robe and put it over his lap. He patted at the ground to his side, looking at Gloria. She stood, wind blowing her hair gently, tall, her arms folded in front of her, thinking, saying a prayer. She shook her head side to side, and the Father answered her prayer if she should stay. She heard Him say to seek truth. She walked to them, shaking her head, then knelt, sitting on her legs at first, then letting herself fall to her hip with one arm propping herself up. She had a look that was disbelief. She sat, waiting. Michael knew her every sign, and knew she was ready to hear him. Elsa had her head on her knees, looking at Gloria, eyes wide in innocence and begging acceptance, a pleasant expression of welcome. Michael smiled.

"Gloria, I understand you are surprised. I thought you were away. I am sorry as this was not expected."

She just stared at him. He glanced to Elsa, then continued.

"This is Elsa. She is…"

Gloria stopped him, interrupting him.

"I know who she is! I comforted her, remember? Satan's daughter? I go have a talk with our Creator and come to tell you of it and here you are, wrapped in the arms of Lucifer's daughter? That is more than surprise. Not because she is his creation. No. Surprise even if she was an Angel of Heaven. What are you doing?"

"Gloria. I understand. I was doing as you were. Giving her comfort."

Gloria shook her head in disbelief, her hair flying in every direction.

"Oh? Oh! Is that a new name that has been made for it? Let me descend to earth and tell everyone go, give comfort to everyone. Speak truth, or I must go."

Michael looked sad, and he patted Gloria's knee. He looked at her and she saw he was as surprised as she was. Leaning back, he looked at Elsa who looked at him with her large eyes, understanding. He put his arm around her, and she fell to his side as he hugged her. He looked at Gloria, who started shaking her head again.

'I know daughter. I am surprised this day. I can only speak true. I was walking and saw Elsa trying to reach for an apple though not tall enough to reach it. I reached one for her, for she said she was hungry. As we talked, she explained she was held by Lucifer, created to get to you, but here only as she was denied love to any except him. She came here to find me because I was the one stronger than him, and she had long dreamed of me. She was made with love in her. When you met her, she had been punished for giving love to another. She was certain I was the only one he could not harm. Elsa, is that true?"

Eyes large, looking up at Gloria, she nodded, holding Michael tight. Gloria looked at her.

"You do not have to show fear as if I plan to strike. If you were lying the Blade would have cut you down by my Father's hand. My father is lonely. He is an easy take as demons call those lonely such. Look at you! You are the temptress! He was not expecting you. Reaching for an apple? Oh, sure. That must have been innocent. Breasts raised to see, that perfect bottom of yours fully out. You resorted to that? And that! The very white silk I gifted you! Oh, that reveals all fully in Heavenly light!"

Looking at her, then over to the robe, she said, "I treasure it."

Gloria scoffed. "Oh, yes? Treasured? I see it thrown off and laying in the dirt! Speak true, or I will cast you out."

Michael knew she meant it. It was the silk she had given her. Elsa had not looked away from Gloria. She said, "I do."

Gloria stood still. She stared at Elsa. She understood that if she was lied to, the Blade would be in her hand. Elsa reached to the robe and put it between her thighs and breasts. She spoke again.

"Gloria, this robe was what guided me. When you Graced me with it, I felt its love. It was Holy. As it touched me, all around me, I wanted to feel that way inside. It came off to feel your father's love. I thank you again for it."

Gloria listened carefully. She heard only truth. She nodded.

"It is now as it was when given. You are welcome. Now, speak true. You are made of desire and temptation. Was there way other to show love?"

Michael looked at Elsa, letting her know he would answer. He looked back to Gloria.

"When we met, I asked the same things. I asked was she not the temptress? The desired one? The seducer? She spoke true. She said yes to all, but then she said a greater truth. That she was created that way. It was not her doing. It was not something she could turn off. Looking at her, even if Angel, is to desire her. She shows love with her form, yes. Gloria, I accepted that, and I speak true. What aroused me and what I made love with was spirit, not only form. She gave both. Even my first sight was of her spirit. It is there right now. Look at her. Tell me what you see."

Sitting still, Gloria looked at Elsa, then nodded.

"I see the one I saw in Egypt. It was why I went to her. Yes, she is showing her spirit. Giving it too, and freely! Father, know this. Elsa, speak true. It will not be good if you do not. Lucifer spoke true when I met him last. He used you to get to me and now here you are in front of me, as there. You are bait to get me. Do you think he created you just to be another demon? Knowing he needed a way to get me? Elsa, again. Speak true. Did your father create you to deceive Michael? To get you into Heaven?"

Elsa sat upright, clutching the white robe tight. She answered.

"Yes. He created me to deceive. To enter here freely."

Both Michael and Gloria were shocked. She was truthful. She had no hesitation in revealing the answer. Gloria paused only a second, then asked more.

"He is an Angel. He knows we trust. And he knows our ways. He would not send you here to have you lie. He is very clever. So, speak true. Did he send you here such where you could say you were deceiving us as it is true, but with that understood, there is more you must do. His wish. To cause us pain?"

Elsa nodded, saying yes again.

Gloria stood, she was tall and glowed bright, waiting for the Blade. Her robe changed to crystal armor. She was majestic and her Wings appeared, filling the valley behind her. She spoke and her voice was as a trumpet.

"Speak true. What is true? Why are you here?"

Elsa looked up at her. She stood up, beautiful naked, holding her robe.

"I am to give my love to Michael. The love true that I have in me. When I have his heart, I am to break it, then leave. Hurt so, my father knows he will be devastated and unable to battle. You will be the only Guardian. He will await my return, then do something, I know not what, that will cause you to appear as Guardian. He will offer you his deal or take you for his own in some way I do not know. I have said all truth. All. I am going to say the most important truth. I am not my father. I am made with love. I seek Michael's love as he is the only one my father will not attack. I want to give him all I am. I do not wish to break his heart. Above all, to you both, I am sorry. I am cursed. Held by this chain around my neck. I have been his slave since made. I want to be free of him. That is beyond true. That is. It just is."

Michael looked in awe. He had never heard such truth. As Elsa said, as none ever had, it was beyond truth. Like the Sun in the sky, it simply was what is. It could be no other way. He looked at Gloria, Wings flapping, lifting skyward. There was no Blade in her hand. Gloria spoke to them both.

"There are chains not wanted. There are chains placed from wishing to please a master. Even if desired, there comes a time any wants release. You spoke true. You are bound by your chain to hurt my father. That will happen if I do nothing. I do not fear your father. All fear my Father. God. I will not wait. Sending you here is crossing the line. He knows that and knows I will go to him. Know this. I will return. God has revealed who I am this very day. I am as none before. Pity Lucifer."

In a burst of light, she vanished.

Scroll Seventeen

Walking to his hovel, Elsa held Michael's hand and asked if he was worried about Gloria. He looked down at her, and felt her concern was genuine. Reaching the hovel, they went inside. He sat on his bed while Elsa took her white burka off, folding it carefully and putting it on a table. Tugging at his robe sleeve, he stood as she took it off him, then folding it and putting it with hers. He laid on the bed, and getting in, she laid next to him, holding him. Head pressing into his chest, Elsa said she was worried; Lucifer was insane. He squeezed her tight.

"Elsa, I know he is. I worry not for Gloria. He knows he can't harm her, so he is a coward and will use the ones she loves. Is that not what you know?"

He felt her head move up and down on his side, nodding yes. He rubbed her shoulders.

"Seeing you here, she understood he could have you be truthful, all the things you said, but it remains his wish to hurt me. That is a way to hurt Gloria, and me as well. One day he will call to you, and you shall be gone. That will hurt me. She saw love in me once more. A smile on my face. I know her ways. But my brother knows that without seeing my smile or my face. With you, he knows I shall be happy, and knows you shall have love. In time, he will call you, command you to do his will, and you won't be able to stop. We will both suffer. Gloria did what is best. Confront him now, stop his plans before more are hurt. Attack, not wait. I agree. I would do the same for her."

Shuddering, Elsa knew her father was beyond evil. Raising herself up, kissing him, she sat next to him explaining her worry.

"When I last met with him, he revealed secrets, asking of mine. I explained my secret was to find any way to be free of him. He told me things that frighten me. He said he would never let me go. That I was to gain your heart. When he had Gloria's attention, he would show a Vision. Show me with you, saying the only thing keeping me from destroying your heart was his control over me. His chain. She would see that if he pulls only gentle on it, I will begin hurting you. If he pulls it with his might, I will destroy you. It is why I was made. He has been planning this since the day of the fall when he realized little Gloria was not with Ethereal. That is how devious he is, and he has only gotten worse. He knows that Gloria will want only to protect you. With me here, the power he has over me, the love we now have for each other, he is certain she will surrender to his lust. Michael, you have seen what he did to your wife with his serpent. Once in her, she could never come back — if only from shame. The serpent, do you know true what it is? What it does? Why Ethereal never called your name?"

Sitting up, he saw complete terror in her. Hugging her, he told her he saw it, but it was true he knew no more than what he saw. She moved back to look up at him.

"Know this. The serpent is the Destroyer. It is poison, like serpents of earth. Its venom destroys love, faith, hope and Joy. One by one. It slithers inside, rising, and first bites the heart. Love dies. It slithers higher and bites the back of one eye. Faith, seeing what to believe in, dies. Then it but turns its head and bites the other eye. That venom destroys hope for one can no longer see anything to hope for. Taking all those, it slithers into the mind, needing no venom there. It hisses, then changes the mind, asking what Joy is there without love, faith, and hope? That is why it is the Destroyer. With his serpent, he kills the heart, sight, and the mind. It is saved for Angels. Humans give those away with no help from him. They are easy takes… Harvest. I know this well. I speak true."

Having a look of deep concern, Michael asked her if Lucifer had done so to her?

"That is why I know all I have told is true. When made, I was begging for his love. I thought the serpent was love as it first appears to be his passion and his desire to be inside a woman. I craved his love, so begged for the serpent to fill me. He forever refused. He created me to love only him. I was not aware of what his serpent was then. On my last visit he said he could never do that to me. If he let the serpent have me, all my love would die, and I would become the Satan. I told him it was horrible to be his daughter and not loved. He said the only thing worse than being me was being him. Sick as he is, he admitted he needed my love and would never have the serpent take it from me. He spoke true. Knowing he would not impale me, and having no love in him, only lust for Gloria, I left and came here. He thinks I am doing his bidding to have Gloria by controlling me…"

Looking at Michael, he saw her as she was. A tortured soul needing love, willing to be cast away rather than deceive or lie to him. Her existence had led to this moment, to him.

"I speak true, I am here only for love. Not him. I have faith, and I have hope you can take his chain from my neck. He will always use it to suffocate my love. He will pull it. When we are one, in Union, he will pull it with all his rage."

Michael was filled with admiration and understanding how much Lucifer had hurt her. He asked what her other Knowing of his evil was. She shook her head in sadness.

"He spoke true of all he will do if he does not have Gloria. I know not how, but he said he was willing to end all things. All existence. Earth. Abaddon. Heaven. All existence. He said he would delight in it. The only reason he has not was his desire to be inside Gloria, even but once. Michael, he does not mean love. He will only use his serpent. He wants no other to have her. He admitted he was worse than insane. Being created in his mind, I know his thinking is far beyond that, as that is what evil is.

Michael, he laughed, asking how could an Angel give up Heaven to create abaddon, live in darkness, give up the love of God, all for your little girl? He spoke true. He said only one beyond insane would do so. With no hope of his prize, all will fall. He is that insane. I ran from that, to you. I could not face the end of all and never be loved. Today, you gave me love. Michael, today I gave my love to you. I love you. I speak true."

They each sat, looking at each other, and each cried sadness and Joy. As their tears subsided, she knelt next to him, body upright, and opened her arms wide. Crying from shame, she shook her head as she spoke.

"Michael, to love you true, I must speak true. Know this, you must know. Oh, one I love. Know what I am, and what I have done. Then you decide if I am one deserving love. I have done horrible things. Things unspeakable. If I must, I will confess each act. I have deceived, seduced, betrayed, ruined all I encountered. I sent an endless line of souls to hell for the pleasure of my father, and Michael, know this. My soul was there. I craved his love, and not having it I loved a demon, as human, once. A fallen Angel you know well. Scorpio. My father castrated his human form to keep him from ever showing me love again. In that way, though just of body, I am no virgin. I wished for love from Scorpio, but he was a true demon. Once healed he left to serve my father. I speak true. I was created to be the purest of evil and have done evil beyond measure. My only worth is that I have love inside of me that is pure, and my love can only be Holy. I am evil filled with Holy love. The love is what I serve. Not him. But you know he is not going to let things be simple or easy for us. I fear what I will be, now, having your love. We must face this. Having love, I do not know if my true love will do to you what it did to Scorpio. It is not about me honoring my father. It is the opposite of honer, it is escape. Gloria saw. She knew. It is why she replaced my black garb with white. That changed me. Now, to be your love, can my black soul be white? It worries me. It should worry you. I speak true."

There before him, arms open, revealing herself, she was beyond anything he could imagine. Heaven and hell. Good and bad. A question and an answer. She was giving the answer. He looked at her and she was indeed beautiful as she had beauty within, and it was not her temptation. He was drawn to her because she was the sorrow she said, yet had hope.

He felt the presence of his Father, knocking at the door to his room. He saw Elsa look at him in awe. Michael bid him enter.

"Father, I was about to visit you, with Elsa. I am glad You are here. We both face sadness, and we have embraced each other's love. Gloria has left to confront Lucifer, saying You have given her understanding. Thank you. Elsa, this is my Father."

She looked at him and her voice was quiet, yet sincere.

"Am I welcome in Your home? I did not ask Your welcome."

He looked at her. He was gentle but certain as he spoke.

"If I asked you to leave, would you go?"

She nodded.

"If I ask you to stay, would you stay?"

She nodded, then smiled, not to be seen, inside.

"Elsa, you are welcome. You would not have entered if not. I ask of you. Do you think your father sent you here, or do you think I called to you?"

Elsa shook her head many times. She looked at Him in wonder. She answered.

"I knew it neither. It was both."

He smiled at her. He nodded, bidding them sit and worry not. He was glad to be with them both. Holding each other, they felt loved, and they listened with hearts open.

"Elsa, after what your father did to so many here, Michael drew a line in the sand where all good souls are welcome. It had to be that the fallen are not welcome here. You are not of the fallen. I want to ask if you know my message to them?"

She nodded.

"It is known to me. It was never said it was all those who fell. I hear the meaning true. Being fallen is believing in what Lucifer believes. If they do not believe that, they are no longer fallen. They are Angel. That only. Fallen is what they believe."

He smiled at her.

"You are the only who has known such and you know this of your own mind. And of that, why do they not know something so simple and so obvious?"

She had no hesitation, nodding again.

"They have guilt and shame. That is why."

He smiled at her, nodding with approval. He continued.

"That is so. Those are powerful bonds to hasataan only they can break. I hope they do. You told Michael of all you have done. Sins. Not against me, but in duty to your father. Do you feel guilt and shame?"

Again, she showed no hesitation.

"I now have sadness for those I hurt. That sadness will be in me always. I can only explain that I have no more guilt and shame than a leaf on a tree for being a leaf on a tree. That is what a leaf was made to be. It did not choose to be leaf. My father created me to be as I was, and that was not my choosing any more than the leaf has. I knew nothing else. I was created to honor Lucifer and fear You. Then, having a soul, though I do not think my father wished that to be, I awoke. I visited my father and told him of my love, and my need to be free of him. Since then, I have not done any of the things I was made to do. None. If I were to hurt anyone now, then I would be ashamed, for it would be sin. I would know guilt. I speak true to You. Love has changed me."

"Do you love Michael?"

"Yes."

"Will you suffer your father's wrath for him. Know this. It will come. It will hurt. You know he will hurt you. Tell, how will he do that?"

"The only way he can hurt me is to part us."

"Is the serpent around your neck only a thing you believe to be real, like the fallen believe in him? Or is it real? Something more powerful than fear holding you to him?"

"Just as abaddon is real, this chain is real. He made abaddon, he made this chain, and he made me. Those are not beliefs. I am not, the chain is not."

Nodding, He stood up and kissed them both on their heads. He looked at them both to show His love, then spoke.

"Love each other. I love you. The chain is real but know that is a belief. Elsa, I have no way to take it from you. It is not your belief, it is his. It is his will, and that is Free Will, just as you have and as all souls do. It allowed you to choose love. I cannot make you love, or not love. I cannot make him hold you or release you.

As powerful as the chain may be, know that your fear of it is his real power. Choose to not fear it and you are free of it even being on you. If he pulls you back, you can be chained to him and be free. He may hold your form; he cannot hold your Will. Know this. It is all I know."

Scroll Eighteen

Suspended in the heavens, Gloria was looking at all eternity.
Although she could be form, spirit, or as was her want, both,
in the heavens and descending to earth she was pure spirit yet
appeared to all other spirits and Children the same as when having
form. Her spirit and body were the same. If she thought herself
having blonde hair, her form would have blonde hair. If she was
happy of heart, her form radiated happiness. Although she could
think herself as something or someone else, she had never done
so. She could choose to look and act like another person, and all
would believe she was so. Such deception was what the hasataan
used. As Guardian, she could see through such deception, and
she thought of Elsa. Gently letting herself drift down through
the dust of stars long destroyed, she let the dust coat her form.
It covered her long legs, her arms, her body, her hair, face, and
Wings. Each particle held to her form, and she knew she sparkled
like the stars in the sky. Willing herself to leave and stand before
the form shaped from the dust, she admired her image. She was
certain she appeared as beautiful to all, and that gave her Joy.
Although knowing all souls were beautiful, she was ever aware that
she was different than others. Born of Ethereal and Michael, she
would hear whispers that she was a gift to those first created. It
was said she was made to honor them with a blessing that would
only be once in all creation. The dream of what all Angels aspired
to be. All said she was the gathering of both Angelic and Divinity.
Blessed, she was given sight to know all that needed to be known.
Everything. She thought such whispers blasphemy as only the
Father knew everything. Knowing none who spoke of such meant
any disrespect, it was praise and wonder.

Thinking back to when she was little Gloria, she walked with
Father to where elk were nurturing fawn and asked if He had
gifted her with knowing everything. He knew that many marveled
at His blessings. Ones given to all, each different, each admired.
He saw knowledge the same as all other gifts given. He sat with
her and watched the fawn, new that day, find its way to stand on

legs thin as twigs, taking its first steps, having no help from the mother. As they watched, He told her the new one had much wisdom. It knew it was alive, new, could stand, walk, feed from its mother, drink, eat tall grasses. He asked her who had given the little newborn such knowledge. She pointed to Him. He chuckled as He shook his head.

"I said nothing. I am amazed to see such knowing. Some things just are. They are what they are. The fawn is a fawn. I did not teach her to be one. I made no gift of such. All around us, it has a name that says what it is. All you see is called nature. Things have their own nature, and what all things are and do, that is natural. Nature has Will, a life of its own. Once created, I did nothing more. The trees, the wind, the elk, the fawn, you. All natural, all a wonder to behold. You have your nature. It is just how you are. I had no part of that."

She recalled asking Him if he knows everything and asking if she did as well. He smiled at her desire to know truth. He looked up to the sky, then His hands, hers. He smiled in a way that made Him seem a child, like her.

"Gloria, it would be a very sad place if I knew everything. Then I would not be in awe of all I see, of that fawn, and you. No, I do not know everything. Neither do you. Wisdom has nothing to do with how much you know. It is often said it is what you do with what you know that makes one wise. That is a nice thought, and it has some truth. I will speak true. I know everything. That is true. I know everything I need to know. If you know all you need to know, you know everything. That fawn knows everything. Think of that. Everything it needs to know, it knows. Look at it suckling from its mother. It knew that. That is a very wise thing to know. I know what I need to know to be Father. I do what I need to do. I laugh if I need to, cry when I need to. I hold your hand to show you I am here with you. That is everything I know. And I know this. You are truly wise as me. You know everything you need to know. If you do not know something, you know to ask and learn. So, I ask you speak true. What do you know?"

Smiling within herself, she looked at the image the stardust, clinging, had made of her. Bits heading off in the winds of the universe, knowing it was once like her, one thing, now another. Her answer that day to Father long ago was that she knew everything. On this day, she knew everything she must do. When needed, she would know everything needed to know about Elsa. Father had later explained that not knowing something is knowing much. The missing pieces, things that do not fit, questions without answers. Those are equal to what is known. What she did not know about Elsa gave her caution. Ones who thought they knew all, or who knew enough of her didn't know the most valuable wisdom. What one doesn't show, what is hidden, those are often the most important to know. She hadn't known her mother had fallen from Grace to save her from hasataan. Any who thought she was a disciple of Lucifer knew little. She ever said she understood nothing of why her mother fell. Not knowing why that happened was wisdom. Unless you knew, heard it spoke true, you knew nothing.

Elsa had spoken true. She had bid Elsa to tell all that must be known, and she had. There was much to know. It was Elsa's nature, as Father said of all things, to deceive. She spoke true she would hurt her father, leaving him. And she spoke true she did all that she wished not to do, compelled such as she was bound to Lucifer. His power over her was greater than her truth. That, Gloria knew. Knowing Elsa loved Michael, that she was tortured by facing hurting him and losing love, Gloria spoke true of what must be done. Lucifer must be stopped. His chain holding Elsa must be broken. His lust for her must end. His destruction of Joy to have her must end. She spoke true that she would stop him. She knew everything she needed to know. He was evil and he had crossed the line. Like the red rose had thorns, she knew she had more then her Blade. She was not yet the white rose. She would remain the red rose in the Garden until Lucifer was no more. Her thorns were her Knowing she must do what is her nature. Keep him from her. Cut him and let him know true the line he crossed offered no rose, red or white. It offered doom.

Scroll Nineteen

"Michael, if you will, tell me of my father before he fell. I know him only as the satan, but know he was Angel. I have never understood how the two could be one."

After the Father left, they had embraced in love again, both surprising each other with the intensity of the passion each had. Elsa had heard many speak of the heights of ecstasy only Angels could reach. If it had been only humans saying such, she would have thought it just folklore. She had heard of wonder reached only in the arms of an Angel, from the fallen. They knew, and had experienced such love, and they told that since the fall they made love no longer, they only had sex. As they told of a thing called Ecstasy, she thought it just another new word, dismissing it as an excuse for failing to be no more than ordinary. Asking them of how it was different, she heard many times it was the spiritual Union that drove form to do things demons or humans could not do and things none could never even imagine. Again, she scoffed. After performing the rite with Scorpio, impaled on his serpent and bursting into flames, as they recovered and he was pouring water over her, she told him of the bold claims made by many of the fallen about Angelic passion being beyond what even demons know. She asked if he had experienced the Ecstasy they kept saying was so amazing.

Scorpio knew Elsa had never been Angel, and saw no purpose in speaking of acts they couldn't engage in. The ritual and having the serpent, though nothing like Lucifer's, was exciting and brutal, better than with humans in every way. It was not what he once had when Angel. He told her that he saw no point in thinking of it, but they were missing it, which he understood. He did too. She asked what he missed, and why did it have a name she had never known. He was careful to not sound too enthusiastic about it but explained it to her calmly and without passion.

"Our bodies are prisons. Even as demons, our sex requires a

form. Our own, or one we take from a human. We can transport ourselves to hell and other places, but we are of body once there. Angels, well, they have what we call sex with their form, and while doing that, they have spiritual sex. Their spirits leave and that is something that is very hard to explain. I'll try. Bodies are about how things feel. Wet, dry, hard, soft, fast, slow. How we look. You know well all that. Spiritual sex knows none of that. The spirit is pure feeling. If we were spirit, I could reach to you and hold your heart in my hand. I could hold your smile. I could be the air you breathe. Like two clouds, reaching each other, we could get inside of each other. And that means we become one. Complete Union. My mind in yours, your mind in me. And we can take any shape or form we wish. A stream of water running over or through you. A light that shines inside. Light pouring out of you. All is possible, and it is never the same. While that is happening, the spirit compels our forms. Our bodies feel those things. It's indescribable. No beginning, no end, no limits. Bodies. I can only think of it this way. It's as if the bodies become liquid. The spirit shapes them to flow in and out of each other. The climax is Ecstasy. The word describes the complete feeling of Joy. There is no higher level. It can only be when spirits make love, when two become one inside. We just rub around on each other. Poke and push. Our bodies are prisons. There is no way out except death."

Recalling she was jealous Angels could have such Union, she still thought it a wild story and wishful thinking. Until this day.

Michael saw her as spirit as she reached for the fruit on the tree. As Gloria was smart to know, she was arching her back so her bottom, as wondrous thing, would be even more so. He revealed he saw why she had pushed it out for him. Why she reached to a tall tree. The spirit inside her was calling to him, it was making her invite him with her form. Her spirit was the attraction, her form held attention. It was her smile, the look she gave, the whisper on her lips. Seeing both, he saw beauty he could not resist. He asked what she saw when looking at him. She simply said she saw strength, his kindness, his excitement, his passion. She stopped and he looked at her, knowing she had just said all the things making his spirit, never even thinking about his form. He was right. She saw all of that, and he was beautiful of form, ever handsome.

As they embraced, she felt elated. It was passion, certainly. Staring into his eyes, she did not will it to be, she felt herself leave her body and he was waiting for her. She looked down, and their bodies were beautiful. She thought how she could put her legs higher, and from outside, her legs went higher. As his arms squeezed her body, she felt his embrace as spirit. The tales were true. She quickly learned how her spirit controlled her every movement, and they did enter each other, two hearts beating as one, two minds thinking the same thing. It was Ecstasy. She told Michael that she was truly a virgin before this day. This is the first time she had made true love and reached Union. Ecstasy.

Hearing Elsa share her thoughts, he wished her to understand that love of body, no matter why, when human or demon, was making love. It could not be set aside as having no meaning. She looked at him, concerned he understood not what she had shared.

"Michael, I know that true for the Children of the Father. The mating, the bond, maiden pride. It is how they seek to live forever and continue to be beyond death. True, you speak of love of the body, pure lust or use, and love of the heart. Affection. I have forever known love of body only. The demon way. More times than grains of sand on earth. Know true. It was nothing but grains of sand to me."

Fully understanding, he wished to share the wonderful gift of their Union. He looked at her, showing only affection and embrace of her meaning.

"It is with my love I speak so. I know that you speak true. A demon knows no love, so such joining has no value. Have you ever considered those to whom you gave your form? Was not the reason to give them hope of true Union? What they thought of as love?

You are very beautiful of form. Was it not to make them feel they were beautiful to you?"

She could only answer it was so. The demon way. He said he understood, and it was taken away or an incentive to be taken from God. It was for that. She stood silent, thinking of the countless ones she knew as nothing more than souls for taking. For Lucifer, not her. She knew no other way. Again, he said he understood. She had been made the deceiver. Holding her hands, he said he must know true, one thing, and it must be asked. Telling him she would answer all he asked, and all she said would be true. To have no worry. He closed his eyes. Then he opened them.

"Elsa, I've answered my own question. Having lost Ethereal to Lucifer, he is not as you, but you are of him. I worried that even with the love in you, and it is love, that you were made such to deceive even yourself. His will to hurt all is to deceive. Give, then take any happiness. I worried if you had thought of that. If the love was put in you to hurt not only me, but you. That is something I worry. You said you know he may pull you from me. To hurt me, but I know if it is love true, it will hurt you also. Then I thought more. Even so, this is real. We could not have Union without love. This is love Lucifer seeks to use. Both, to have my daughter. I wish we were new, and nothing else. I have given you my worry. You could not have me if I did not give all I am to you."

She had been crying as he spoke. She kissed him, and said she was open, and wished to have him know all she was, so nothing would be between them. She reached to her throat. Holding the serpent, saying that it was there, and the thing that would ever be between true Union. She had a look of such sadness he knew that it was, and that to hear it was to be hurt more by it. He said he wished to hold her hand, walk from sadness. To see places free from sorrow. A walk. In peace. Before, he wished to be one with her again as he felt close and wanted her and he spoke true. She looked as his passion rose, held it with both hands, and with joy said he had much to share.

Talking of her father, and her nature, she found herself taunting him as when she took humans. It was a shocking to her as she couldn't stop herself. She did not wish to do anything other than give him her love.

Holding him, she was compelled to look at him and ask how many have known his gift. He was proud as he told only Ethereal other. Laying on his thigh, looking, she started laughing, at first gently, then seeing his questioning stare, she laughed more, harder. He asked if she knew of something she could share so he may join in her laughter. Taking one hand away, holding with only one, she was unkind.

"I really spoke too soon. Perchance not enough to share, and not enough for many. Just one. I'm sure you've enjoyed it fine on your own."

Her laughter grew, and it was a cruel thing to say as it was not what she thought in any manner. He looked at her, clearly confused, surprised and hurt. Her laughter hurt her ears. Even as her face turned to a look of desperation, then fear, the laugh continued. He watched, the look on his face became confusion, then great concern. She was not able to stop laughing, and began striking herself, then when that did nothing, she pressed her hands hard over her mouth, her eyes crying from fright, not from laughing.

Without knowing why, the laughter stopped. Her eyes grew large, and she kept her hands over her mouth. Tears continued to stream from her eyes. After a long wait to be certain the hysterical, maniacal outburst had stopped, she took her hands and grabbed him, hugging him with all her might, begging he understand she was sorry. She meant nothing she said, nothing was funny. Holding her, he waited. When she first giggled, he felt her spirit was repressed. He knew the words were not hers. The laugh was not from her, and it was a shock only as she was aware of it as well yet had no control over it. After she gathered herself, she knelt next to him, her face looking at him, and it showed intense sorrow and pain.

"Nothing, nothing, nothing was from my heart. This gives me such fear. I hurt you! I am so afraid you think that was my mind. No. No, it was not me…"

He nodded gently, saying he knew it was not her, the voice was not her own, it was his brother's. She began nodding. A glimmer of hope returned to her eyes, and she was able to calm herself to speak.

"Yes, that was him. His manner. His taunt. Before I left, he had commanded that I do more than leave when you loved me true, he told I was to humiliate you. Say you were nothing compared to my countless lovers. Laugh at you. Michael, it was unstoppable. Hearing the words, feeling the laughter, my body shaking from it. And wanting it to stop so, if near a cliff I would have jumped off to have laughter no longer. I thought my love could stifle his commands. That I could stop. That scares me. My only comfort was you knew it was not my voice. Thank you for such careful listening. It was most cruel. He told me to do such, and I heard him say not do so many times. Only when I had your trust. I know it was a simple command. It is done. I had thought it just a comment, how I should be thinking, like him. I did not know he commanded it such, or I would have warned you of it. I can recall nothing else said more. Can we still walk? Do you still have love for me?"

Looking into her face filled with desperation, he was quick to say of course they would walk. Do all things together. Then told her he had much to tell her before any other thing. His look was most serious. Her eyes widened, and she showed great worry. He moved her shoulders down to have her lay flat on the bed, then took her legs and pulled them apart, putting his face to her perfectly smooth mound, and before kissing her there, said that he had much to say.

Later, as they took their walk and she asked of Lucifer, she said now knowing Ecstasy, how the spirits join, she worried that was what he would seek from Gloria. Though the most beautiful of any in form, her real beauty was her spirit. That was what her father sought to have. To have her soul, not just her stunning body.

Michael said that was so. Though Lucifer fell, he was the one who retained all Angelic gifts, including ecstasy. He saw it the day he cast the fallen to hell forever. The day Lucifer took his serpent and thrust it into Ethereal. He defiled her body; the spirit's venom taking her Joy and hope as she described. He saw him take her spirit. He stopped and was unable to speak for quite a while, and she led him to a log to sit. When able, he looked at her and was devastated.

"Elsa. She had a pure soul. Beauty, such as Gloria has. You as well. The spirit inside shapes form. On that day, I watched as he took her beautiful spirit, all she was, and ate it. He threw her back soulless. I have no way to describe how horrible that was. He has her spirit. It's why she has never called out, why she can never leave…"

Hugging him tighter than she thought possible, she understood. She felt the pain, and she cried with him. Her mind racing knowing Lucifer took the souls of all the damned. He consumed them. His strength came from taking the life of others. For the first time, she fully understood what horror that was. To take all anyone had. He was the word evil. He was sick. He could tell she had gained understanding of the true nature of evil. She had been made a demon, but she was not as him. She shook as the full truth of her chain flooded her with agony beyond measure. She fell to the ground, wailing and in fear. Michael regained his strength and held her, begging her tell him why she suffered so. She was gasping but had to tell him. She grabbed at him, kissing him with true emotion and love. She took a deep breath and sat on the ground where he had joined her. She was grabbing at her serpent collar.

"Michael. Love. This is a nightmare. On this day of reaching Ecstasy with you, I know truth that is beyond all terror. All this time, I thought this chain was a leash to pull at me, pull me away from any I love. Drag me back to him. No! No, Michael. If it were only that, then I would cry Joy. Know this, for now I know. Michael, this chain is tied to my soul. If he wishes, one pull and it will be torn from me, his to eat. He eats souls, just as he did to poor Ethereal. Michael, that is how he will hurt you. His plan all along. Oh, Michael…"

She was convulsing in pain and torment. She could not be consoled. He held her tight, wanting her to find comfort in his arms. When she could cry no more, she sat up and looked at him.

"Michael, I worried not coming here. I thought he wished me to entice you and lust for me, then wished me to leave and deny you my love. That would hurt, but I could let you know, as I have, that I would do all to stay. That it was his wish, not mine. That no matter what happened, you have my love. You do! But that is only heartbreak. When you told what he did to Ethereal, I saw true. His plan is to do it to you again. Again! As I stand in love, in your embrace, this chain will do more than pull me back. It is bound to my soul. You will watch the love I have for you, my entire being, my soul ripped from me, and he will eat my soul with its love for you in it. I will just be this prison in which it is held. I will be nothing for he will take my heart and soul from you with one pull of this sick chain. Shaped like his serpent. He will steal my love from you. If you hold on to me… oh, oh, no. No! That must not be! You must not hold me! If you hold on to me, when he rips my soul away, if you are holding me tight, oh, Michal! Oh, wait… if he knows we are in Union holy, in a state of Ecstasy, your soul will be one with mine! Your soul shall be torn away, with mine! He can have mine, but no, no, no, never, not yours!"

From pure love, Elsa pulled from him, running away fast as she could so that Michael would not risk losing his very being to the hasataan.

He Who Devours Souls.

Scroll Twenty

Scorpio was sitting having his serpent worshiped by a daughter of a false god who wished to do the most unholy thing she could. Telling her she had found the right god, kneel and be a sinner. Although he had rarely used his serpent for such easy takes, castrated, until he could beg Lucifer to repair him the serpent was more than needed. Casting the simplest spell on the women kneeling before him, they thought the serpent was just a very large human cock and were not able to see his wound. None excited him, so the serpent was a mere garter snake in size. It was hungry and best not to let out fully. He kept it behaved but needed his parts as they were tools of his trade.

Not asking the girl to disrobe, she had started removing coverings while she sucked away, thinking it would impress him. Like most any young one, her body was fresh and unmarred, and she was certainly impressed with herself. Once naked she managed to turn herself around to be facing away from him, her head fully back, her body arched so the serpent slid into her throat easily. Leaning back such, her nipples pointing up, and she was rubbing her breasts her whole body was held in place by the serpent in her throat. It had gone on long enough. He did not need to watch the acrobat act from the market. He began asking the questions that would commit her soul to hell. He knew she would have a hard time saying anything in such a position so he would tell her to raise her hand to say yes.

His den was dimly lit, and he had many pillows for his long hours sitting while sad ones sucked their existence away. Having just gotten dark, that was the start of most any demon's day. Looking down to the girl he noticed she had a glow on her belly and breasts. It confused him as the door was closed. A sense of fear came with the glow. He knew. Looking up, there stood Gloria. She was not blazing light, which he knew was more frightening than if she was. She was in full armor, the crystal a second skin, clear yet having all colors as was the nature of crystal. Her hair was full, framing her head like a helmet of the most savage warrior. Her chin was down, her eyes able to stare into his. He had known Gloria as friend when both were Children, and he knew her manner. She had not come to talk or ask how his wound was. She was there for battle.

He did not hesitate. He knew what he needed to do. He pushed the girl away, giving her command to leave, casting her clothes over her so she would not linger gathering them. As she ran out, Gloria paid her no heed. Keeping her eyes on him, his serpent sank back in his lair. He started to wish her welcome but a force powerful as a blow to his jaw shut his mouth. He sat, in fear for she began moving objects around them to block all openings. All manner of things were flying about. When all was finished, she stood still as a statue. She was showing no glow, but her pupils were glowing blue. She was seeing truth. Her head wasn't shaking or nodding, and her manner became more menacing as she stood watching him, not moving, not speaking, all sound ceasing from outside. He knew that she had stopped time. None would know anything that went on between them.

He understood she wanted him to sit there, to think, understanding why she stood before him. He had long been in his sad work and he posed no threat to the Divine. She had never visited him before, though he knew true she had appeared, giving Elsa a tonic for his pain. He did not understand that either. Knowing only Gloria was listening to his thoughts, he had nothing more than fear. She was most certainly wrath, yet he knew he not worthy of her attention. He was able, in mind, to ask why the Guardian had appeared.

Gloria did not raise her voice, yet it was a force that pressed him hard into the cushions as if a mighty wind. She held her stare, and that too had a force of great power. She finally spoke.

"What presses against you is truth. What you do is lie. This day, speak true, Michael not Michael. Why are you here?"

His eyes widened. He did not understand. She had saw what he was doing. He started to speak but was instantly pushed back with even greater force.

"What you do was seen. What you do was not what was asked. Again, why are you here?'

He was afraid, even more then when Lucifer had castrated him. He was aware of how Angels speak but had not spoken such for a long time. He thought of the question, then answered.

"I am here to do Lucifer's command. That only."

She remained still, certain in manner, eyes bright blue, armor reflecting the glow from them.

"On this day, you choose to remain Lucifer's fool. That your deeds are his, not of you. Know this. You do your Will. You have a choice. Stay or leave. If he were to destroy you, having left, forsaking him, you would be Home. I speak true. You obey only your mind, not his. I appeared when you were sliced with scythe black. I gave the girl remedy, for you. On this day, she has asked to be in Heaven. She is there. Lucifer's own, not here, doing harm to none. On this day, you are here, casting those weak to hell, not guiding them to light. Speak true. Can you not leave this?"

Her truth was more than he could face. He began sobbing, saying yes, over, and over, he could leave. She did not relent.

"Then, go."

He cowered before her, frozen, then when able, he cried out, "I can not. I can not!" He would not be wanted after the fall. She spoke with truth that went into him as if spikes.

"If Lucifer's daughter was welcome, and I said plain, go home, do you think I lie?"

That scared him more than all else. He looked up at her, desperate.

"No. That is not what I think. I belong here. I have made my choice. There is no way to return from it. I speak true. I speak true."

She was not interested in what he thought, and told him so.

"You spoke no truth. You said what you believe, not what is. The only truth was saying you made your choice. If you choose Lucifer, you remain damned. If you choose Heaven, you are welcome. Father gave you that choice, ever. It has never left you. Know this, I have given light in your darkness. I can do no more. What you do is what you do, nothing other, and concerns me not. Stand. Now."

He found himself rising, though he had not attempted to. Her words felt as daggers in him. He doubted. She was before him.

"You will always be where you choose. I am not here for you. Your master has crossed the line. He harms one embraced by Father, and he has intent, true, to harm me. On this day, he will stop. He will respect the line forevermore or he will meet my wrath. He will be no more. I wish you to call him. He cannot see me. I will never be in his sight again. If he will not come, then I will hold tight to you and descend to abaddon with you. I speak true, if to abaddon I descend, you will be first in the path of the Blade as it will down all in my way to him."

"I will call to him. I will call to him! I know not if he will come."

She looked at him. She saw he was afraid but was speaking what he knew. He was not important to Lucifer. She told him what to call out.

"He will come. Call with despair for you have news of Elsa."

Trembling, Scorpio understood he was being used the same as he used so many women. He meant nothing to Gloria or Lucifer. His head suddenly was suffering from Gloria's voice, louder than his own mind's thought, filling him with panic.

"Use you? You believe true you are being used by me? An innocent like the ones you use to feed your master? I know true you do. You are now pure demon, lost. I will do such as you think true. You shall be never Michael. Nor Scorpio. Do not call the satan to tell news of Elsa. No. He will come from a call being news of you. I shall call you what you now call yourself. Victim. You shall be such now. Used."

She was no longer seen, but he knew she remained there. He heard the world again. Sounds and smells returned. He called to her, but no answer came. He kept calling. She had warned him he would be a victim, and when his door burst open he knew she had answered. Two large men had burst in and they stared at him on the floor as he had been kneeling, begging for mercy. Both men were shirtless with massive muscles, and each wore a leather flap not much longer than their hips, and nothing more. One was bald and seemed hairless, the other was bald but had a thick beard. They had slammed the door behind them and after looking at him with nods.

"Told you he was all pretty-like. Too pretty to be here all alone. Let's give pretty lad some good company."

The other grinned, his skin tight and glistening on his muscles. He nodded, saying, "If company be what you wants call your dick up his ass, then make it double the fun. What say you, pretty one?"

Not waiting for an answer, they wasted no time using him as he had used women. Unlike him thinking the women plain or unattractive, they thought him pretty and took pleasure filling him. Pulling him to be on his hands and knees, they entered him fully. No working their way in. He felt blood running down his thighs but could not beg for mercy as his mouth was filled with a massive cock pushed down beyond his throat, in fully, never pulling out enough to allow him to speak. They were relentless and each came in massive surges, but kept going, still hard. The one in his ass asked the other, "How sweet be that mouth?"

"I had me some better, I have, but sure looking forward to that sweet ass. Trade?"

He heard the other one hum.

"Tight as a schoolboy, it is. Gots it alls ready for you! Let's flip him over, see what he done got on top, hey?"

Pulling out of him at the same time, the one behind him kicked his hip and he fell to the floor. He was unable to shout or even move. He lay trembling. They pulled at him to lay him on his back. The one who had been in his ass stared, saying, "Hello? What the fuck is this? A fucking girl? I dunno see no hole, but dunno see no pecker either. What the fuck? Is he one them hermaphrodites you have to pay so much for?"

The other knelt to look. He shook his head.

"Oh, too fucking bad. You had me hopes up, you did. Naw. Just had his pecker took off nice and clean. Balls too! And we was going to do that very snippy to remember us by. That is a fuckin pity. Well, we can make a hole there. A little slice. Make it all sweet-like. Have his first period, he will, but I won't mind no blood when I ram him hard. Sick fuck you are, I know you like it. What you say? Ready for some virgin treat? Thought ya would. Hand me that knife there. That will do just fine. A nice straight slit for the new girl. There. Sweet and ready. You be the first. I'll pump his ass and meet ya inside."

As Scorpio was about to pass out, he saw his blood splatter a bald head between his legs and two large smiles of delight. As he started to see black, he uttered,

"Master..."

As he finished calling the name, he heard each man scream, then gurgle. Barely able to lift his head, he saw Lucifer standing between his legs, a man in each of his hands. He had grabbed them by their throats and had them dangling in the air, his arms raised. The gurgling came from his choke hold. Their faces were turning purple, their eyes bulging. Feet flailing, Scorpio was growing weak from being cut open, doing his best to be heard, calling to Lucifer a faint, "Dying. Bleeding..."

Looking down to him, Lucifer removed his hands from their throats but they remained suspended in the air, still gagging, still gasping as he had only removed his hands, not his strangle hold. He looked at Scorpio, then asked how they made a hole fine as that? Putting his hand over the wound, saying it would be the only time and he would fix his problems, he would need to work around the clock as payment. The blood stopped and Scorpio no longer felt he would pass out. Using his arms to raise himself up, he looked, and his parts were back, looking normal. The cut had vanished, but his mouth, throat and ass hurt worse then when they were going at him.

Lucifer ignored him, knowing he was fixed, then turned to the two brutes hanging in the air. He held his chin and nodded. He shook his head, looking at them suffer. He spoke to them.

"You are exactly the type of men I am always looking for. You know what you want and take it. No guilt in any way. Yes, I can use you. If I let you dumb fucks live, will you serve me?"

Still gurgling, they both managed to spurt out a pleading, offering a cry saying yes. Lucifer nodded. He smiled at them then asked, "Do you know who I am? The yes means nothing if only to save your life. You are making a deal. Your life in exchange for serving me, forever. If that is agreeable, say yes again, and say my name."

The first man, the one with no hair anywhere, said, "Yes, satan!" Looking at the other man, the one with hair covering his face, he said the same. Lucifer smiled, adding he appreciated their enthusiasm. He turned to Scorpio, telling him to rise and stop being a weakling.

Scorpio knew Gloria was watching. She could not be seen, but more frightful was that Lucifer, who could see spirit, could not see her. He realized, wisely, that if he looked her way or said she was there, or even showed fear, Gloria would strike him down. He heard her say "That is truth" in his mind. He walked up to Lucifer, who was waiting for him. Looking at him, he told him they should be rewarded for signing the contract.

"Yes. They should remember who they now serve. And, after the fucking they gave you, I think you should give them equal pleasure. Scorpio, I think I shall have them serve you. Now, you will need ones out grabbing takes as I want you harvesting without stop. They'll be fine. Have them pull takes off the street as they pass by and toss them before you. Yes, that will do. You know true, your serpent will make you their lord. Let it out. Here, I will get them ready."

The two dropped to the floor, showing terror as they had no control of their movement. Flicking his fingers, they were lifted to a kneeling position. Another finger flick, their heads and shoulders smashed to the ground, both their asses up in the air. He looked at Scorpio.

"If ever two were ready, it is the ones before you. I hear them begging for the serpent..."

He looked at them, and each began a fearful begging, crying.

"Serpent. Please. Take us. Fuck us. Please."

Lucifer was delighted. He turned to Scorpio, most pleased.

"Let it out as I bid you to. Oh, give it to the one who cut you a new hole. He deserves it most."

Filled with fear, knowing Gloria had just said he was free to do what is right, he had a choice. He could do what Satan demanded or say no to the command and beg Gloria to send him home. He heard her voice.

'I said your choice was made. You said you served this vile monster. Not Father. Do not look towards me."

Her words were truth. He knew she would not save him, though she would strike him down. Shaking, he commanded his serpent to grow. He stood, waiting. He was in a panic. He was so fearful it was not hearing his call. Lucifer looked at him. His eyes grew angry. He looked down, seeing but a small worm poking out. He looked back at Scorpio. He was in disbelief.

"Oh, how pathetic all fallen are. Can't even rouse the snake to do the assholes that treated you such. What am I going to do with you? Will you be able to get that other worm up for the takes? Oh, if you don't, I will snake them. Oh, I should do you too. I really should. What the fuck? Why can't you release the serpent, anyway?"

Shaking, he grabbed at his ass and crotch.

"I don't know. All I can think about is my fucking ass. That fucker tore it open. It fucking hurts!"

Standing with his arms folded. Lucifer rolled eyes, then nodded.

"Total Angel, still. Precious little ass. That can be fixed. You two, each night, get hard and enjoy his ass. Next time I see him, I'll want to see you both in his ass at the same time. Scorpio, when they do and I watch, your serpent better shoot out and smack them down. Do you all understand?"

They all shouted out a loud, "Yes, master."

Lucifer nodded, flinging his fingers at Scorpio who went flying to his cushion, happy he survived. He had a full view of Lucifer. The demon smiled and laughed as his serpent came forth. Though not as monstrous as when he became the full hasataan, red with scales, horn, and tail, he was not holding back. It was gigantic, the room barely large enough for it even as it spiraled many times to fit in the space. The two new minions were screaming in terror knowing Lucifer was going to fuck their asses with the beast. Lucifer continued to laugh, taunting them, having its head face them, its forked tongue flicking in and out, licking their faces, leaving scars at its spit scalded their skin. Scorpio could smell the singed flesh, hear their screams, thinking only he was thankful it wasn't him Lucifer was using for his pleasure.

The room was dark, but there was enough light to see the serpent slither to the first hole, lick it, hear the scream from being burned, then thrust only head deep. Pulling out, it went to the other and did the same. The two had no clue to how that was nothing. In them fully, it would weave through them, its head exiting through their mouths then out a good way, would turn around to stare into their eyes, hissing. Then the serpent would lift up, flick them around the room, impaled inside, next biting venom into their faith, hope and heart. It was a horrid act and he cowered from it though he had done it with his own serpent many times, but to Elsa for pleasure leaving her unbitten.

As Scorpio watched, Lucifer was absorbed in feeling their pain and of taking their souls as the serpent was about to bite. With his attention so focused, he paid no attention to the shimmer that grew near him. Scorpio could only notice it as it was an arc of movement barely a ripple of the air. Then, to the side of Lucifer. The ripple became a blinding arc of pure light, slicing down with unreal force and speed. It was a force that shook the entire planet, all thinking it an earthquake, all trembling in fear.

As the light dimmed to where its havoc could be seen, the sight was unimaginable — but most unimaginable to Lucifer whose wail of pain was heard in Heaven, by all on Earth, and all in hell.

Lucifer was on the floor, grasping his groin, black blood spewing from a giant stub there. He was writhing in pain and was in shock. The two minions had vanished and not there. In front of Lucifer lay the still slithering, now twitching serpent. Its head did not know what had happened, where to go or what to do. It bled black blood where it had been sliced off the hasataan.

Standing tall, majestic, Gloria could not be seen. The Blade floated in the air glimmering countless colors of light. As the Blade moved directly over Lucifer's head, pointed straight down at it, its light revealing his face hideous in pain and fear. Gloria was but a force, invisible to all, mighty, having no fear, and the Blade was floating in the air to have the most direct path to strike. It remained above him. Letting its eyes adjust to the light of the Blade, his snake had found where it bled and was licking up its own blood. What seemed like eternity passed and Lucifer had used a hand to shield his eyes then moved it away as he groaned one word.

"Gloria?"

It was a question. He had no clue she was there and had not expected her to take first action against him. She was only a voice. She spoke and all about them shook from the force of it.

'I am Doom. Are you in rapture? Do you lust for me?"

The Blade remained in striking position. Lucifer reached to his gaping wound, shocked it was there. He looked and saw his serpent lapping up its own blood, then his head fell back and he screamed in agony.

"What have you done?"

It also echoed to all eternity. Gloria offered no reaction. The Blade hummed in anticipation. It was ready to strike an eternal blow that would cast him endlessly, without stopping, to nothingness, the darkness God had left for any deserving such fate.

The sword rose higher in a manner most certain. It was a beam of pain into his eyes.

"The Guardian does only what is promised to any who cross the line in the sand. You crossed that line to take a child. I speak true. You must tow the line. Do you wish the girl now? Without your vile serpent?"

He laid there, in fear, saying nothing in reply. Lucifer watched as the blade moved closer to his head. Its light was more frightening than the power of the Blade for it held much worse. It held Gloria's wrath. With no warning it became a circle of pure light. Swung so fast, it was seen only as a blur, a wave of light appearing, then gone, back to the form of the Blade, aimed straight down at Lucifer. Gloria's voice bid him look around him and speak true of his power to take her now. It was a command, and he could only do as she said.

Looking around him, the blur of light had been of the Blade in duty. The serpent had been sliced into infinite nothingness, now only pieces, a serpent no longer. The speed and might of the Blade had burned it to ashes. Lucifer was surrounded by nothing more than gray dust to be swept away. He lay crying; his tears enraging Gloria. Her voice cut as sharp as the Blade.

"Cry? You cry? The tears of all you damned are real. Your tears are nothing. They stop now. The line is now from your eyes to your cheeks. If your tears cross that line, the Blade will strike. I speak true."

Lucifer froze, not knowing how to stop tears, but his fear stopped them, not his regret. Gloria was relentless.

"I commanded you speak true. Once more. Answer me this. Do you wish to have the child?"

He looked up to the sound of her voice, in fear. The Blade raised with full intent.

"Answer with the bold way you told all you would take a child. You will not answer whimpering and shaking from fear. What is there to fear? The Blade will not strike down truth. Only lies or harm to an Angel of God. Speak bold with your arrogance, your might, the supreme power you tell all you possess. Answer me only in such manner. Do you wish to take the girl? Have her? Defile her?"

He showed no response, creating more ire in the Guardian.

"Stand with your pride, demon. I command you, stand up, speak true, with your might. Say to all what you will do to a child."

Raised upright, the blade to his right above his shoulder ready to slice away his head, it hummed letting him know it was ready to strike with all its power.

"Standing before all… The fallen, Children, demons in hell and in all places, speak true as all will hear. Do you, mighty hasataan, wish to take a small girl, a tiny child, happy, playing in Heaven's pasture for your lust? To defile her Divinity by force. Rape? That is what you made as your promise. You have power only to rape a small, sweet child. It is still what you desire, mighty hasataan.

A small girl with a smile and trust in her heart. Do you wish to take her?"

Gloria spoke for all in existence to hear. He looked at Blade, and simply said,

"No."

He cowered, expecting the Blade to strike. He looked at it. It would have struck him if his answer were not true. His expression was blank. It was the first time he knew his madness. All he had done, what he had become. He faced truth. He had never really wanted her. It was something he had convinced himself of long ago. Gloria saw his mind and she did not stop. She prayed the Blade be merciless.

"You say to all, most so yourself, you do not wish the girl? Answer true. That may be so now as the Blade shows no mercy or reasons. My question will go to lust for the Holiest Angel, Gloria, throughout all time. Answer me this. Speak true. Did you ever want to have Gloria?"

This time he knew the answer. He said, "No."

The Blade did not strike and remained at the ready.

"You speak true that you never wished to have her. You have ever lied. To all and yourself. One last question. Answer me this. Speak true. If not to have Gloria then or ever, all know you are a liar, but the Blade is at your neck and it will tell the truth if you do not. If not lust for her, why did you fall from Grace? Take Angels with you? Create abaddon and corrupt Father's Children in the Garden?"

He had no hesitation or fear of the Blade as he answered.

"I lusted only to be God. All I have done? All done only to steal

His power."

The Blade dimmed. It could still strike him down, but it told he had spoken true. It remained aimed at him in striking pose. A light shone on the Blade from above, and it absorbed into it. Without the Blade moving, Gloria's voice spoke.

"Your Father is merciful. He seeks not vengeance such as you alone lied telling it was what he would do. A lie most profane as you know not what He will do. He bid the Blade stand down, not finish you or cast you to eternity. The Father gives all His Children a chance to use their Free Will to understand the mystery of their soul."

Lucifer looked into the emptiness, knowing Gloria had been stopped from striking him. A look of innocence was all he provided, and offered no thanks. Gloria waited, then lost all hope of his admission being more than words. She looked at him, and could only speak true.

"I speak only His wish, not mine. Know this, for it is the Will of your Father. Knowing you need time to understand your own insanity, He banishes you for a thousand years to pray and to find light for you are truly lost. You are in total darkness. He asks that I visit you when that time has passed, and the Blade will be with me and what you will see, never me as you do not deserve my visage as it is Holy. I will ask if anything in you, even a passing thought, wishes His Grace, or if you desire to hurt any of His creation ever again. The Blade will speak true. If you continue to seek what you have, you will remain another thousand years, and I will return with the Blade to ask again. I will ask until no such wish is in you. It may be a thousand years, or all eternity. I care not. Look at the Blade. Speak true. Do you understand His command?"

The Blade was dim as he said he did.

Gloria then asked if he thought his banishment was just and showed the true love of his Father.

The Blade remained dim as he answered.

"Slut, whore, hiding from me, embarrassed as you are not worthy of my gaze. Hideous such none will ever fuck you. Oh, most unwanted virgin, no, it was not just. Like you, His banishment is shit. So none may ever see such a withered hole, it is you who must be abandoned there. Then all will have Joy as none will see you ever again."

Gloria let his words be heard by all. She spoke to all his fate.

"Free no more until you are Knowing of your folly, know this. You speak true as you remain opposed to all that is good. Know this. Your Father is God, Almighty. He has taken all your power. All you had was ever His, given to you in love, and you used it to harm all in creation. Denying such gifts, you now have no way to Will yourself to any place. Know this. I speak true and warn all. None will be able to reach you as that is His Will. Any who try will meet me, and I will hold the Blade to them. You, and this is ever just and righteous in all ways, are banished to where you planted the seed of Elsa. A place known to none but you. None other. She knows not the way. God commands all are denied there, or to even think of that place. To think of it will be sin. None will go there, only me though I rue the thought. Know I will go only to honor the Wisdom of the Father. I take you there now. Know this. I speak true. You told all, bold, lustful defiler of child, you wished to take Gloria. Think in your thousand years of how you never took her. It is you who are pathetic. It is repulsive to be near you. I have no wish to take you as I wish not to see you, hear you, or know your name. You will feel my disgust, feel my power, but never see me. You are banished, by me. In the name of the Father."

Scorpio sat, staring at nothing, Gloria had taken Lucifer to exile.

He knew not what to do, or what would happen to all who followed the demon. A young girl knocked on the door. No minion opened it. She knocked louder, and he was sore afraid to answer.

Scroll Twenty-One

Looking over their favorite valley, Michael opened his arms wide as he could as Gloria descended, her Wings filling the sky, her armor fading away, her hair flowing in rivers above her, a simple linen robe forming around her. Standing, waiting, he was filled with his love for her. As she reached him, her Wings flew off her, each feather of light going its own way, filling the sky with patterns that formed birds who flew to the heavens, becoming stars that night. As the Wings flew away, she landed into his arms, and they hugged. Squeezing her with affection, he was filled with her happiness, her with his. Turning, he held his hand for her to hold and they walked to their hovel.

Telling her he had made fine bread, had collected her favorite fruits, even shelled nuts and baked them in the sun, she said that was good as she needed all those gifts. It wasn't a long walk, and she said she had a gift that was being delivered that will arrive a bit later. He said he needed nothing, but a gift was a treasure, she nodded to him, saying her gift was indeed such, one he would treasure always. He smiled and thought of what it could be. One thing he learned of Gloria, though all Angels could know each other's thoughts, Gloria was able to keep a secret as her secrets were never actually hidden, just respected by all as hers alone.

Eating with passion, she asked of Father and told how He had given her a gift that made her strong in dealing with her uncle no more. He shook his head as he admired the way she dramatized such things. The confidence of youth was something to be cherished. He asked what she had been given. She explained how Father had taken her to the Garden and showed her the new flower. He was fascinated. His expression revealed it.

"It was a single flower, just one sitting atop a long vine, nestled in with others. It was true beauty. Red so deep, velvety, dark and lush, shaped like, well, as shapely as a certain daughter you know, being beautiful and perfect in form. It had so many petals, tight inside, more and more all around until the petals curved slightly outward, the outermost ones giving view to the ones ever growing inside. It was a wonder to see, and its smell is like none other. It will be cherished always. Holding it under, quite small, were deep green leaves shaped as the petals, hugging them. She said it started small, all bundled snuggled tight when new, and as it grew, the petals opened to form the beautiful shape no other flower has. Let us go there tomorrow to cherish it."

He loved her description, and he was open with his impression.

"Daughter, I must tell you, I know you convey what you saw most correctly, but not knowing it was a flower, I would say it was someone describing you."

Gloria looked at him, her eyes glistening as she took his hand, thanking him. It was much more of a compliment than he could ever know. She squeezed his hand saying there was more. He nodded, waiting.

"He told me that being the most beautiful, such are often taken, those taking it think like most flowers there are many more. But, for now, I am the red flower. The only one and it has a way to protect itself from being taken. He told me to reach to its vine to bring it close to me, which would allow me to see and smell it close. In the dark of the stems around it, I found its vine and as I touched it. I was grabbing barbs that pierced my finger and thumb. I was stunned. Other plants had no such barbs. He stopped my bleeding and told me to but look at the stem. Pulling the other flower stems aside I could see the tall stem had the barbs all along it. Leaving it be, I asked him what they were, and what was the beautiful flower. He said he gave it a special name. A rose. I asked why such a name. With His look of it being so simple, He said he had watched it rise, and now it had rose. He said the armor on the stem was also new, and He named those thorns, saying they were named as they looked like tiny horns. It would become known well in days ahead. I said I understood how such beauty would be desired, and the rose to keep its beauty, truly, found a way to stop others from taking it by having thorns. It was new. Perfect beauty, and a warning to respect that beauty. I told Him I felt much as the rose. Oh, father, He said I speak true. With that He lifted me so high and gave me such strength…"

She had tears as she told him how much it had moved her. He told her it was good to be moved so, and he had an idea of what was meant. She waited to hear him speak of it.

"I am sure, from all you told me, that He said you were the rose in this Garden. Everything you described the flower as, you are. As Guardian, you have thorns to give warning, and ward off all evil intent. Gloria, I think He made the rose in honor of you. He is an artist. Nature is His canvas as we all know. Thinking of you, there in my stead, He thought of you and his brush painted what He saw. You. A rose. Daughter, that is praise most high. It will be in many places and cherished as love and beauty forever. You will touch so many. He will share it with all as inspiration. That is His way. I will go with you tomorrow, give thanks, and see it with the inspiration. What a gift."

She sat and said a prayer of thanks for Michael and his love. He was her inspiration in all things. Having finished their meal, he asked her how she was after her confrontation with Lucifer. She shrugged slightly. She said she could speak better sitting by the water. They went outside and she drank water, as did he. She held some in her cupped hand then let it fall through her fingers.

"It is done. I decided he did not deserve seeing the beauty of me that is truly both you and mother. He had no right to see what he wished defiled. He only spoke true from that. The one who threatened to destroy all was afraid he would be destroyed. I learned much from that. The same as his saying he lusted for me. Inside he knew he would never have love from anyone as he was sick. To feel powerful, he claimed he would pluck the rose. He said he would take it as he knew it would never be given. Then he admitted he was a coward, and it was feeling powerful he wished, never me. He wanted the keys to the garden. I don't know why, but he didn't understand it has no lock. Father, it had to stop, but it was sad, and he is very sick. As I took him to his abaddon, coming back I had a knowing most troubling. We shall see if it is prophetic and pray not. It scares me."

Michael saw the worry in her face. He said he would share her worry. She nodded.

"Leaving him, I heard his insane laugh, and he called out saying it was far from over. Then I was filled with Knowing. Putting him there will do little. He is not the last hasataan. He is the first of many. Ones forever more. An army as insane as he. The battle for souls continues, forever. Such total damnation from but only one hasataan... It has changed everything. Forever. We have Heaven. Think of all those who live in hell. A slave girl, a king, a daughter, a child, a warrior, all, and father, this you know most true. A wife, and a love…"

Gloria began sobbing, falling to him, grabbing hold of him. He hugged her. He was alone, but he had Elsa's love. He cried with her, and the tears were true. They were sadness. She gathered herself and looked at him. She was able to wipe her tears, and his, then speak of pain.

"Father, of all things you have ever done, that I have ever seen or known of you, nothing has given me more awe than offering your love to Elsa. I know nothing more giving than that. It has touched me like nothing else, ever. If you can, tell me what happened. How she left. And, of your heart, now. Only if you can. I can wait forever if that is what you need."

Looking at her, he knew she was the one who would understand. The Father knew what happened, but Gloria understood how he felt. He looked to the road, then back to her.

"Gloria, she is much more than any will ever know. She is Elsa, and she has touched me, and I love her and will always love her. Neither you nor I had need to hold the Blade to her and it never appeared. She opened doors that had no keys, giving me love and only truth. She knew they were the same. Love without truth is not love. Created, not born, taught to be evil beyond Lucifer, she found love inside, saw it the only light she would ever have. Do you know what she did with that tiny, flickering light inside of her that brought her to me?"

Gloria could only look at him, waiting as it had to be a wonder. He stared at her, his eyes crying.

"Gloria. This has changed me forever. In the dark of her life, she took that one flicker of hope, that one flame, and she gave it to me."

Gloria was stunned. She saw him moved and he was both sorrow and Joy. She said to him, nodding,

"She was true. She found her love and loved you."

He sat and his head went side to side. He had the sweetest, yet saddest smile she had seen ever. She asked if she misunderstood.

"Daughter, yes, that, and far beyond what even now I could imagine. Yes, our spirits joined in pure love. We were one. Her love was real, and beautiful far beyond what a form could show. She gave herself, fully, and she cared for me. I know that as she gave her happiness to save me. She surrendered herself to love. That is love. As we joined in ecstasy, she had no understanding of it but once we became One, only then she realized the power Lucifer had. It was her. She was his way to pull my soul from me and consume it as he did to Ethereal. I saw the knowing awaken in her. She grasped the serpent on her neck, and she realized it did more than hold her love to pull her away from me. No. As she told how he consumed Ethereal, she shook in terror, realizing the serpent was chained to her soul. He would rip her soul from her, and she would be to me as Ethereal is, just the shell holding nothing. The memory of her beautiful soul…"

Gloria sat horrified. She could not speak. She was stunned. He held up his hand, a sign there was more.

"That shook both of us. Then, she went where I could never even imagine. She is beyond wise. I am still reeling from seeing her think all things through. She held the chain, thinking of her father's evil. She stopped and looked at me with a look of terror, then the saddest expression that ever could be. She knew what it was. He created her and made sure she wanted love and could give it. He chained her soul and held its grip though she thought it only held her form and kept her from any she loved. Then she connected all things. He hated that I had love, had Ethereal's love, your love. Not able to fight me as I had the Blade, he had his own Blade, the most powerful one ever. Elsa. He couldn't strike me or harm me with the Blade in my hand, or yours. He didn't want you, he wanted me! To destroy me. Knowing by claiming he would take you she saw how loved you were by me. He knew she would come seek my love. He allowed her to come, even told her how. He knew I couldn't be seduced or fall for a deceiver. He knew she would offer her love for real. He would let her have my love. When he got your attention, he planned to have you watch him hold my soul in his grip, offering to let you save me if you surrendered to him. But he would take you, keep me, and consume us both and not care what happened to Elsa. Knowing that, she looked at me and said he could rip her soul at any time. Then, she figured it out. Lucifer understood that when we joined in Union, Ecstasy, our souls would become one…"

Gloria sat, her eyes wide, and finished the sentence.

"He would pull the chain and he would take you. Yes. And I would come for you. He would make his offer, and Father and all Heaven would be left unguarded. He knew all ways in, and he would seize Heaven. Father, that is beyond knowing. Please, what happened?"

"Gloria. She was as incredible as you. Only you would be able to embrace it all and have the love to do what she did. As I reached to join her in Union, she figured it out, saying that was the only way he could take me. She got up, saying she must protect me from him. We could never be one again, never unite. She ran and like wind, she was gone. To save me, and as she knew, you as well. All of Heaven. Our Union was the only light she had ever had. It was her salvation, all she ever wanted. It was everything to her. That I know. Nothing is hidden in Union. She gave up love to save us all. I knew I could not follow her or ask that she stay. She had lived in fear. Here, with me, knowing? That would be fear beyond all fears. I could only let her go. I will be hers forever. She gave herself to me, I do the same. In everything that a soul can give to love, she did. She gave me her heart, her faith, her hope. Her joy. The very things the serpent you slew kills, she gave to me. I hold them now in my heart. She will never have them again as long as he exists. I cannot explain or show how it feels to have her beauty in me."

Gloria looked at him, crying. She pleaded.

"Father, God took his powers. She is free. Go to her!"

He got up and hugged her. He looked at the water, then the road, then back to her.

"She knew you would seize him, and he would lose his dominion. Gloria, this is the part that hurts most. His powers are not simple. As our Father tells us, there are things even He cannot touch or change, or give. He cannot make me love you or stop loving you. He cannot make you feel what you do. He can inspire. But will, love, loyalty? No. He cannot take those as they are ours. Elsa, in all her Knowing, realized the serpent, his chain, was not a thing. It was the bond of father to child. She could not escape being his daughter. He could not escape being her father. That is a power that cannot be changed. I don't fully understand it yet, but she did. I saw her realize the chain could not be broken. No matter where he is, that tie will always hold her. I know this, no matter what, or when, if I meet her again, if he remains, even if she pleads my love, does all she can, I will show none in return. I will not put her at risk. Ever."

Standing, he took a deep breath. He looked at Gloria, smiled, and said what he knew.

"If we should meet, she will know. My not responding. My turning away from even a sweet hello? That will be telling her how much I love her. As much as I want her with me, that is how I protect her."

Gloria saw her father as the most majestic Angel there would ever be. As she hugged him and wept for both, they heard a bird, one formed from a feather on her Wings earlier. It was circling above them. It carried a small bundle. Reaching up, the bird dropped it in Gloria's hands and flew away. She held it and cried clutching it to her breast. She managed to say it was her present. Then she dropped to the ground, holding it on her lap. Michael knelt in front of her and waited. After a long time, she looked up, and said it was something she could not comprehend. It was sacred. She held it and told him where it was from.

"Father. This will haunt me forever. It came when I went to where Scorpio dwelled, where I waited as he called to Lucifer. He was fearful to summon the hasataan. I could only show Scorpio he must summon the dark one or face my wrath, showing him my ire had begun as I sent all objects in his abode flying, striking him, and creating need for Lucifer's protection. This, what I hold, flew into my hand as all else crashed. He called out, knowing I would never relent, and Lucifer sent two lost souls to Scorpio, and both answered his call with Lucifer's wrath, much harsher than being struck by trinkets that I had used. Scorpio was raped by two unholy men, and as Angel I could not serve the demon. It was then I took a feather from my Wings, made it a bird, saying to bring it to me here, in Heaven. I wrapped it as a gift, and with string for the new bird to hold it tight. The bird flew all the way here, giving it now."

Gloria handed him the small rectangle package, wrapped in simple parchment. Looking at her, he gently unwrapped it. He stared at it, and he was lost in what he saw. After a very long time, he held it to his heart. He had no words. His face said more than any words he knew, and he knew all words. Looking at her, they stared at each other. Much time passed, and they knew it was more than a miracle. Gloria moved to sit beside him. She told him there was more to know. It was greater than what he had seen. Only half the story. He shook his head in disbelief. She nodded, letting him know she was filled with Knowing.

He held it out so both could see. It was a drawing held in a frame, simple in nature, sketched in charcoal, a portrait of Elsa. It showed her exactly as she had revealed her soul to him. Her form and spirit were both there, as one. All things, sacred and not, we're in his hands. Before his eyes the mystery of being, the portrait being made from shadow and light, was the beauty of all things. He knew it was the most precious thing he had ever known. Elsa. Looking up, into his eyes, into his soul. It spoke and told of her longing for complete surrender to love. She was telling him she was all things. Seducer, temptation, innocence, seeker, and sweetness. He had been shown that she had given herself to love, and her face was asking for what she had never been given, her message being that she was hopeful when there was nothing to hope for.

Gloria told him there was something equally beautiful on the back of the portrait, to see all he would want. Look deeper. Beyond what he saw, to know what the artist revealed. He need only take her portrait from the frame.

Looking at his daughter, nodding at her, he was astounded there could be anything more as the drawing was truly Elsa. There, before him. The soul he loved. He carefully removed the drawing from the frame and turned it over. On the back, in simple scrawl was written, "the key"

Under that, the artist had signed his name. It said,

"boy"

His mouth hung open. He shook his head as the words were a mystery. Gloria told him what must be known.

"On my way back from banishing her father, I was compelled to go to the lair of the wayward Angel. Scorpio. He feared me and said Divinity bound him to the banished one. I could only speak true that he could be chained to a pillar and be free. I had no answer, and I was not there to save or destroy him. I told him I had the picture of Elsa and commanded him tell who made it. He cowered, saying only this. Boy, one having no name. In his eyes I saw a boy, a seer, one sitting in a tent in the vile marketplace. I needed nothing more as birds from my Wings guided me to him. I took form same as all there, not Angel. The birds circled above a tent that had no markings and was unadorned. It was there I met the boy, only six, and he was on the ground with only a rug and a small bowl for coins having none. Seeing he was true; I knew he waited for me. He bid me welcome, calling me Malaka. Father, I veiled my Angelic form to all, him most so. Then, asking him his name he said he had none, he was just a boy. I spoke kind to him, describing the drawing, asking if it was he who drew the pretty one, the one most small. He told me, in his words, "No, not little, big, like Malaka." He pointed to me. I asked why he gave her the name, The Key. He was certain. In his words, he said, "She be key, key be her, picture, her, one thing." I asked how he knew such. He said to me, in his words, "One only drew what one saw, only gave name one knew."

Michael looked at the image of Elsa. He said that the boy saw true. Elsa was a question and an answer, and she was the whisper on his lips forevermore.

Gloria sat, looking at him, knowing Elsa left him destined to ask questions that have no answers. Then she finished the story, telling him the boy had said, in his words, "In all things, know the space between." Knowing her father was ready to hear, she said the boy revealed that between them was that which held them, bound to each other, as the parchment in his hand held both sides of what must be.

He understood, and he looked at her with his acceptance of the message. He said the wisdom would guide him and knew it would guide her too. He was shaking his head, thinking, then asked her of the boy.

"You see only true. The boy, human, only six. He explained her with such sight. It was love that bound us together, and love is the key. Elsa is the key. I wonder, if I go to the boy, how would he draw me?"

She then told him that would be a mystery yet would be his key. Just as the boy saw her true as Malaka, he would reveal what one could know. He nodded, saying that he wished such Knowing, but asked why she said how the boy drawing him would be a mystery. Then she told him.

"Father. I speak true. The boy. He is blind."

Scroll Twenty-Two

Running to the desert that was the edge of Heaven, the gate of Paradise, Elsa passed the oasis that welcomed all entering, but would be the way to leave, never to return. Looking back many times, she understood Michael wished her to be safe from her father's hold. They each protected the other by surrendering to love. For them, love would be the sacred Union they had on the day her father was banished and revealed to be beyond redemption. She would forever be bound to Lucifer, as he was her father and creator. If she was one with Michael, her father would rip their souls to join him in the true abaddon, the one where *He Who Hated All* dwelled. To love each other, she and Michael could never have their Union, and never know Ecstasy again. That would be the gift of their love to each other. To be apart.

Knowing he was not behind her, she stopped at the entry to Paradise. It had all things of beauty. She had run past mountains, forests, plains of grain, volcanoes, and places with shapes she never knew existed. As the green of grass surrendered to sand, she was at the place all who entered would be cleansed of all folly, and all notions of what they once thought they were would be washed away. It was a sight of such Majesty she wished she was but a human, a child, flawed but welcome, the wonders of Paradise waiting for her, the Vision ahead, Michael's hand, held out for her small hand, longing for the love within her.

Standing, she understood she had that. All his love was in her as he had given himself to her and he would be a part of her forever. Her thoughts filled with a vision of her laying on him, looking into his eyes, feeling how she poured her love into his mouth, how it filled him. A simple thing, but it was everything she had. Her every part was filled with what she was, and she was love for him. Filling her mouth with her spit, it was what she was. It was of her, from her, and the only way she knew before reaching ecstasy with him, to put herself inside him. Looking at him, pressing his mouth to open, she filled his mouth with her life. She saw his eyes. He understood. He knew. She told him that now she was a part of him. Now, he had all of her, within him. His blood, his form, and his heart. She was inside of him.

She held herself, feeling what she now was. He had filled his mouth with his life, his being, his love. From above, like an Angel, she put her mouth on his, and took all from his mouth, filling her being with his. As she stood, her arms tight around her, she knew she was in the arms of Michael, forever.

Seeing the desert circled the flow of the life of Heaven, a river of Grace, it reached the rim of an endless cliff that surrounded a crystal blue lake, cascading to fill the lake as a waterfall that said to all that they were in Paradise. The river flowed white once over the edge, and it splashed white as it reached the lake, sending sprays of splash, and the splashes flew up, not as water, as white birds that flew up and created messages of welcome in their patterns of flight. All around her was awe, it being beauty, and it was holy.

Standing looking at the place all would have as home if evil never existed, she cried. Her tears were from knowing she had only known evil, something made by one, her father, He Who Destroyed Joy. She thought long of the abaddon, the black place he welcomed all those who had fallen, and all who followed him. It was where she had dwelled since created. A black, endless cavern, its levels never ending, casting the damned deeper and deeper as more flowed from its river that was hell's waterfall, splashing black, a rushing torrent of souls that hit hard black stone. Those sad souls stood confused, forever only lost, their only welcome was eternal suffering. Satisfied being given so little when they had a chance to ascend to Paradise, they thought fornicating with only lust, denying God, killing, stealing, raping, warring, using others, worshiping fake idols, gold, hating all good, and wanting only to be granted vile pleasure was a fair exchange for eternity in the pit that waited for them in hell. It was her father, as serpent, who tempted the Children, giving them sin so they may join him in abaddon. She thought of how pathetic her father was. He had shaped his true self to be a serpent that was so large it tore anyplace it slithered apart. She shook with repulsion as sin had made women crave the serpent, lusting it be large, filling them with what they thought was pleasure. Craving the largest serpent possible, no such creature filled them with love. It deceived them, denying ones who had only love to fill them. Those who craved ever more, ever larger serpents would soon meet her father. He would send his serpent inside them, their eyes in awe, begging for it to enter. It would. Then screams of excitement were replaced with screams of pain and terror as the serpent grew inside of them, ripping them apart, tatters of remains flying to the line of women who thought they alone were the one who could engulf his serpent, her father laughing at them and all waiting in the line. He laughed more as it was endless. When created, Elsa thinking the serpent was his love, she had begged for his serpent to take her. She had been made to think such. Now, she was Knowing. She knew just thinking of such insanity would cast her to her father's side.

Thinking, she was filled with something that quenched all desire for she thought of Michael. How he had no need for serpent, had no sin, nothing that would harm any others. She had found Ecstasy. Love was not a serpent or sin. It was the touch of his hand on hers. The warmth of his breath. The pleasure of his smile. He, like any human man, had more than enough to fill her with pleasure. With it came his passion, his desire, his Knowing her beauty was the look in her eyes, the whisper given to him only, the way her mouth opened to kiss him, the way she wrapped herself around him and held all that mattered. Him. In him, she had everything. In him was the love for her. In her, he had everything, for he had her. In her he was given true love. That was all any needed. It was what she had in his arms. They would be around her forever. Her forever around him. She had reached Heaven. She thanked Gloria, for she had taken her black and made it white. Gloria had shown her the key to Heaven was what she was. Inside. Gloria had simply handed her a robe that made her beautiful. The robe lit her darkness, opening her eyes. Seeing Gloria, she saw what Michael had created. Gloria was Majestic and so kind that she lit the road to her own father, Michael, for the daughter of Lucifer. Gloria showed her the gate was open, the key to Michael's heart and love was the love inside of her.

To give Michael all her love, she would deny her father what he created her to be. She would never be the next Eve. The serpent would never deceive her. Heaven would never be her father's garden. She would fall from Grace, taking the key to Paradise with her. He would never have her, and she was the only key. If he pulled the chain and tore her soul, that is all he would have. The key was her love, more than her soul, more than form, existing only in Union, only in the Ecstasy of real love.

Smiling, thanking Gloria, Michael, and God, she stood at the edge of the cliff, cast off her robe, then dove into the waters below.

Scroll Twenty-Three

Floating above all eternity once more, Gloria thought of all the ways Lucifer had tried to have her, and failed. She thought of Elsa, and her very being began crying, filling the universe with sorrow never known before. Bright stars faded, comets stopped their travel, little chipmunks on Earth looked up to the sky knowing sadness more than hunger. She thought of Ethereal, and wept more, this time to herself for none to hear. Her mother had guided her each day, even though long cast to nothingness. Such was the power of her love that it remained in Gloria in all she did or thought. Ethereal's love was eternal, and that was what none other knew.

Watching a new star come into being, she thought of her father, Michael. The day of the fall he became new, and in her eyes shown brighter than any star ever made or to come. His love lit the Heavens for her, and all who were good. She longed to be like her mother, but she knew she was most like her father. A Guardian, and lonely, without a love. Knowing not where Elsa was, he was without her for now, but he had Elsa's love, which was the most Holy she knew of. Elsa was truly something new. She was the reason the Creator gave all things Free Will. She began as a demon, and was now a Holy Angel, but Gloria thought her more than an Angel. She was more than that. Not of God, not born of woman, made to know wrong as right, she rose above all such beginnings to be the Holiest of all, for she was the Angel of Love.

Willing an image of herself in the ether of nothingness, she saw her beauty and Grace, her long blonde hair flowing in the winds of the cosmos, her face now looking much like Ethereal. She was the Holiest, and the most Beautiful One ever to be, but she sighed as she longed to be a young woman with no Blade, no battles, no warrior armor. She wished to be an Angel loved, one in Union with a holy Angel who loved her innocence and kindness.

Lucifer would be away for a time, but that was little in the scale of eternity. He would plot and plan, and the battle was far from over. He would be back, with more than vengeance. His time away would be like a caterpillar of Earth in a cocoon. He would emerge as something new. More powerful, more devious, more determined to have her.

Having grown from the red rose with thorns to protect her, she was now the white rose and needed no thorns. Her telling the Creator she would be the true Guardian, to protect all who suffered from evil, had made her the Guardian Angel all prayed for. With the Blade of Glory, she had the power of her Will to strike evil wherever it existed, though she knew it could not be done by her alone. Evil had spread to all places, and even without Lucifer guiding it for a while, it knew no stopping. New minions would seek to rise to power, and sin and pain would seize the moment to shape new hasataans.

Jumping on a strange flying creature from a planet newly formed, she stood on its back and let her hair flow behind her, wondering where the creature would take her. As she rode through the stardust, she thought of what she needed to do now that she was Guardian.

Heaven was filled with many Angels, some who had lost parents or Children in the fall long ago. There were others who idolized her campaign to stop all harm or hurt. Her first task was to call to them, asking them to join her in defending the new line. To be there whenever evil ones wished to harm or hurt someone, to cross the new line she drew. She would tell them she wished an army to defend the innocent, and they would become Guardian Angels to each living soul, no matter where. She was certain they would rally to her call, and the balance of good and evil would change forever. The day of the Guardian Angel would be in tribute to Ethereal, and her father. It was their goodness that made her exist to protect all like them.

As the army of Guardian Angels formed and brought sanity to all things once again, Gloria new her true mission was to find Elsa. Thinking she had suffered more than any other, she had been wrong. Elsa was the one who suffered more than even she could have imagined. She had cast herself to her abaddon to save Michael. That was love supreme. Elsa was alone again, and so was her father.

Gloria knew one thing.

Elsa would be found, and she would be in Union with Michael once more.

Jumping off the flying beast, her Wings filled the sky above Heaven as she descended to cheers and shouts of her Glory. She was home only to raise her army, and to tell her father not to worry. Landing at the door of their hovel, her Wings flew apart, each feather going to an Angel she thought would be a powerful Guardian, and became a Blade in their hands, acting on their Will for stopping evil. There, standing, was Michael, his arms out to welcome and hug her. After his embrace, she looked at him with a determination he knew well. She was Gloria, and she had a mission.

"Father. Know this. I speak true. I shall form an army of Guardians, and they will be under your command."

Looking at her with surprise, he was confused, saying he thought she wished to be the Guardian. Lowering her head to look him in the eye, she nodded.

"I will guide them, but I have a calling that must be answered…"

She rose off the ground a little ways, held up her right hand with one finger up. He knew she was issuing a proclamation.

"Father, know this. The next time you see your daughter, you will also see your love. I go to find Elsa. I will not fail…"

With that, she lowered to the ground and took his hands in hers, and quietly asked him a question much like she did when little Gloria.

By T. Ulick   205

"Father… Elsa is one hot demon. Do you think she can teach me to be a temptress?"

As she ascended, her Wings forming once again, Michael stood, smiling, then laughing, watching her fly away. The Creator was there, standing beside him, watching her fly away with a large smile, and His respect.

"Michael, that is why I think Gloria is a wonder. In seeking a love, she knows who to ask for help. I think Elsa wrote the book on that one…"

Epilogue

"I wish to thank you."

Wearing low-cut jeans not jeans, gauze top not gauze top, neither were fabric but rather a Wish to be jeans and top. The jeans looked tight as skin as they were just the idea of what jeans should look like, just as the wisp of translucent gossamer flowed as if in a wind as it was only what a gauze top handmade in India should look like on a tall, thin and beautiful Angel with flowing blonde hair who dressed and talked like a hippie from the '60s.

Contrasting the tall Angel's fully revealing barely-there look was the simple black knit sweater that hinted at what was beneath, a long black dress without pattern that flowed gently revealing more of what was under, but neither showing much more than a small form that needed to be studied to understand the mysteries it held. The once demon, now Angel, was shy. Her beauty was timeless. If she spoke, it was most often with her eyes. Dark brown as if to be black, her eyes were her true attire and all else hid what was for one only to see.

With the small one was a man who wore a simple white linen top without a collar, and loose cotton pants of the lightest cream color, tied at the waste with cords of cotton that formed a belt without a buckle. Barefoot, he was not as tall as the hippie Angel, yet far taller than the little Angel he held with his arm offering gentle love. His hair was long enough to be call long for the times, and it had a mix of browns and some grays, simply tossed as if combed by hand, for it was.

The tall Angel was leaning with her back to a man who was smiling at her pose, enjoying how she was using him for support with her arms crossed in front of her at waist level, a rare moment of looking shy and timid as he knew her to be anything but those things. He was wearing a simple muted green tee shirt, second-hand shop jeans and boots, his grizzled hair neither long nor short, and he had a short beard that was a mix of brown and gray, though the gray was white in many places. Calm, confident, and having his cheek resting on top of the blonde hair that was blowing all round him, he was rubbing the Angel's upper arms with affection, and with each reach down to her lower arms her eyes closed and a ripple was sent through her gauze top.

"Dude, did you hear what she said to us, or are you too deep in Angel dreams to reply?"

The little one smiled at him, knowing he heard her. She moved her eyes to the tall one, and waited for her full attention.

"Gloria, he is Knowing. I was not yet finished. My thank you is not in my words. Words mean nothing."

Looking up at the man holding her hand, Michael, he nodded.

"Gloria knows that. She's just fishing for a compliment about being his dream come true. You know she is young and foolish enough to think he's the one who had his dream answered. It was her dream that was answered."

"Dad! You said it yourself. I'm like the greatest catch there's ever been. I mean like, hey, I know I'm your little Gloria and all, but facts are facts. I'm hot."

Looking up at Michael, the little one nodded with certainty.

"She speaks true. She is."

Shaking his head at her, he couldn't disagree.

"Elsa, yes, she is beautiful. And spoiled. And now she's reading your sex advice scrolls and I think those are going to her head.

Gloria. What scroll are you up to?"

Reaching up to rub the beard resting on her head, Gloria gave her most innocent smile and looked surprised. She began counting on her fingers, making a pout with her lips, a serious expression as if doing calculations, then nodded.

"Number 71."

Elsa tugged at Michael's sleeve to let him know to lean down so she could whisper in his ear. His eyes widened as she talked to him alone, his eyes growing even wider as they looked over to Gloria. She tugged at him again, and he looked into her eyes as she gave him a kiss. He lingered once she was finished, looking into her eyes, love pouring from his into hers.

"Father, you're standing in front of the holiest of Angels. Please, innocent eyes here. I was hoping you could restrain your lustful ways."

All heard a voice that was not expected. Walking up the stairs to the large back porch of the mountain estate Michael and Elsa had made their home was the Father. He had said he would visit the new Evergreen, inspired by his cabin in Heaven, and though surprising everyone, they were filled with Joy seeing him even if Michael hadn't finished all the moldings and cabinets.

"Gloria, you need to throw that dictionary of yours away. What was that I heard you saying to the choir last week? Ah, wasn't it that your handsome beau said you were just a plaything for his lustful desires? Really? Was it he who said such?"

With all eyes on her, Gloria knew she had to speak true.

"Well, perhaps it was the excitement of the moment, but Father, we left HBO on, and perhaps it was that I heard…"

The eyes stayed on her, and she looked at the Father and was trying to keep dignified as she admitted it was something she had shouted out.

"Yes, I will admit I shouted out that I was just a plaything for his lustful desires. I learned it from Elsa's *Secrets of the Seductress* book. Scroll 37, advanced secrets for being desired."

Elsa smiled and nodded knowingly to Michael, then the Father, proud of her top selling book that had taught Gloria to have confidence. Held tight, Gloria was still feeling that she was not as attractive as Elsa. The Father looked at her, and asked her why she worried so.

"When the dude helped me find Elsa and get that serpent off her neck, I was fine until I heard you and my dad talking about her while you were standing in the grove of apple trees where they first met. I still can't believe you two were talking about what a sweet bottom she has and how he couldn't resist taking a bite out of her apple! Dude, you're the Creator and all, but you didn't make that bottom and you were rockin' on the fact she was back to sneak peaks at."

Elsa stood, smiling, looking at Father and nodding thanks, then Michael, nodding once more. Then she looked at Gloria and said it was true, she did have one.

All except Gloria broke out in laughter. Elsa walked to her and reached up far to rub her cheek.

"I think the same of you. How could I ever be as beautiful as you? You are the first Angel. The highest apple on the tree. The one I could not even reach the lowest apple from. It is you who changed my black to white, who embraced me where I could be uncovered and loved for my heart, not my form."

Rising up off the porch, she reached to where she could look into Gloria's eyes. She leaned forward to kiss her, both hands holding her cheeks, and with just her thoughts said it was why she wished to thank her.

Staying in air, she turned to the Father as he walked to her, and she kissed him, and thanked him for being a true father to her, for she had never had a father to love. Letting herself lower to the porch, she turned to walk to Michael who was already missing her in his arms.

The one holding Gloria, a mystery to all, finally spoke.

"Yes. I am a mystery, even to myself for I awoke far away from Heaven, and there I explored what is beyond what even He knows. I was like Gloria, alone. I know now that the one insane had to rise. It could never be where that would not happen. One had to learn what Free Will was, and stop the sick child Lucifer. He was that one. Gloria is the light and the way for all to see. From where there was nothing, I saw her light blaze as she stopped him. He truly was the deceiver for he did not return to his abaddon. He lied. He never escaped to his madness, his mind."

All except Gloria looked at him with shock. Faces filled with questions, voices not able to speak for the news was beyond belief. Elsa grabbed at Michael, then her throat. The Blade of Divinity appeared in Michaels hand, and the Father stood motionless, staring at him, at a loss for words for the first time in all eternity.

Moving to stand next to the new Angel none had known before he appeared with Gloria, bringing Elsa to Heaven free of the chain and her prison, she held up her right hand in proclamation as she rose slightly above them.

"Know this. I speak true. Fear not. I had cast Lucifer to his abaddon to contemplate his harm for thousands of years, but not to cast him to nothingness. He vanished, true, but not into himself as it appeared to have happened, but to the place beyond where things end. Where he once fell to rock bottom, he Willed himself to be above all things where he could plot his return, watch all that was to be seen. He was not finished with his evil. He was just starting."

The new Angel watched her with admiration. She turned to him, telling him to speak true. As she lowered herself, she hugged him and said it was his story to tell. Giving her a sweet kiss, he turned to speak once again.

"I was Created in nothingness. I was never in Heaven, but found myself floating in a place where there was nothing the day I came into being. I knew nothing of time, or stars, or other Angels. I knew only that I was. That I was there for some purpose. In darkness I dreamt of light. Alone, I dreamt of one to be with. I didn't know more than I was something in the nothingness. The thing I learned is that in the dark, it isn't dark. It is a place without light. Then the most incredible thing happened. I saw a thing. I know now it was a boulder. It was drifting from where things Created by the Father floated where there was once only dark. It was far away, but I was forever changed. I wasn't alone. I wasn't in nothingness. I thought of wanting to be on the rock, and I Willed myself there. Just that. A thought of being on the rock, and there I was. It was not a thought, not imagination, not a dream. It was hard and solid and I knelt down and cried. I have no idea how long I knelt there, but I needed to cry, and did. Then, I saw a light. Do you have any idea what it is like to see a light for the first time? To be in the dark and then see that?"

The Father laughed, saying he had a bit of a clue what that was like. They smiled at each other.

"Now I know that our Maker began as just a thought and that He created light. I didn't understand that until later. I was in awe of the light heading my way, but at the same time I was afraid of it. It was something I had no way of understanding. I Willed myself off the rock, backing far away from it into the blackness of the endless nothingness, but not too far to see what the light was…"

Turning to Gloria, he gave her a look of love that all could feel and share in.

"It was Gloria. It was something so incredible I didn't know what to do. I thought I was the only one who existed. But there she was. A streak of light going up and up, and when she reached the place where there was nothing, the place I was from, she put each arm out to her side, put her head back, and she let herself fall the other way. Down. All I could do is try to understand and I wanted so much for it to be real, so I realized that just as with the rock I Willed myself to, I would Will myself to follow her. I was afraid. I worried if she knew of me that could be a good thing, or upsetting to her. She was all alone, and I felt that she wanted that. She did. I sensed that. As I followed I saw all that had been created. I had no idea that there was a whole universe. There were endless wonders, but nothing as wonderful as Gloria falling, changing to be head first as she broke through the bottom of where things made nothing below. Abaddon. I watched from the hole in the top of it, and saw endless beings circle around her, and then the evil one rise from the black stone to meet her. Then suddenly she flew up back to Creation and the evil one followed her. I didn't understand it all, but I knew inside she was light, he was dark. I stood there, and suddenly I felt a rumbling on the top of abaddon. I looked down and the mightiest of his minions began to swarm in the hole, weapons in their hands, serpents hanging from them. An army of new hasataans. All ready to follow Lucifer to the Arch. I learned what the Arch was later, but at that moment I only knew inside that they wanted to seize Gloria."

Stopping, he held up his hand to indicate he needed to take a pause, his head down. Michael looked at Father, then Elsa, finally Gloria. She was standing tall, looking happy, waiting for him to continue. She spoke to the others with her mind.

"Pretty cool, hey? Wait to you hear the rest!"

Having gathered his composure, he looked up again and continued his story.

"Now, yes, I understand all the things I didn't then. All I knew is that the demons were about to fly from hell and go after Gloria, my light. Then something I still feel happened. I rose up, far back from the entry to hell, and found myself clad in armor, and I had a light in each hand and they were so mighty I can not describe them. They were bolts… lightning bolts. Pure power. They reached up beyond what I could see, and they were just as long reaching down. I rose up high to be able to use each end of the bolts, and as the demons flew out of the top of abaddon, I wielded the bolts. I was a blur even to myself for I was turning in a circle, and with each turn I struck endless demons and they vanished into vapor. I have no idea how long I fought them, but it was a long time. At the end, when the last of his army was vanquished, I descended to the entry and all that remained in abaddon were weak underlings crawling or running in fear. I looked, and the bolts were gone, my armor vanished. Not knowing of Heaven then, I rose to seek Gloria but she had turned to Heaven, and I kept going up, finally far enough to land back on the rock where I had started from."

Gloria took over, looking at him first, smiling, telling him she was impressed with how well he told his story.

"You know the next part. I taunted my uncle at the Arch, then eventually found Elsa then all the lovey-dovey apple picking and hot sex in the grove with my dad. Then she ran off and I promised to get her back for my love-struck pops and all. I needed to think about where she ran off to, so I Willed myself up to where everything was empty, to that last boulder. Yep. Meant to be, destiny, and Elsa doesn't even have a scroll for that one… Well, she does have number 243 which comes close, but it was no chance encounter. I rose up, and there he was! Yep, looking at me like a puppy with those big eyes all smitten with my beauty. I mean, hey, of course he did."

She started laughing, then as he smiled at her, she looked at him.

"Or, was it me who looked at you like that and was smitten with you?"

Holding out his hands for her to take, he assured her they both looked at each other that way. They stared at each other for a long time, and Father, Michael and Elsa all knew to let them show their love to each other. They were all amazed, and it was beyond all knowing. Not even the Father knew what had happened.

The new Angel looked at Gloria, chin down, eyes into hers, saying it was good to share what happened next. It was the most important thing of all. She nodded, and turned back to finish the story.

"On that rock, that place where nothing had ever been, we made love."

Elsa burst out in tears and ran to her, hugging her and kissing her, so proud of her. Michael was on his knees, crying, letting it all sink in. He had worried she would never find a love who understood her and loved her for what she was. She had. He looked at Father, and he was shaking his head in awe, tears on his face running down. The new Angel stood tall, knowing that all told was a surprise, and even he understood it was a moment Gloria had long waited for, just as he had waited in darkness for her. He walked to Michael, and held out his hand to help him to his feet. No words were needed. Prayers said long and true had been answered. Father wiped His eyes, then went to them, saying it was most unusual, but He had no words for His Joy. It was a mystery, but more than anything it was wonderful. It was all He had hoped for Gloria, and much more.

Turning to Gloria and Elsa, they waited, and Elsa was Knowing. She looked at Michael and getting a nod, turned back to Gloria and asked if she could tell of what happened to the hasataan. What of her father and need they worry more with such news. Gloria smiled at her, then rose up and stood by herself to tell of what happened next.

"I thank you all for being so kind to me for all the time I was alone. And Father, to know that I had to be the Avenger, the Warrior true. For the Blade. I needed all of that next…"

She raised her hand, and a Vision appeared floating in the air for all to see what happened as if there. It was a Vision so powerful it shook the mountains where the new Evergreen was, and the sounds filled the valley and beyond.

As they saw the two Angels embraced in each other's arms making love, behind the boulder they all saw Lucifer slowly rising up without a sound. It was a shocking moment for Lucifer saw the one he lusted for being loved by the new Angel. The look of wrath on his face made all of them shudder, most so Michael. It was far more vile than when he saw him the day he became the hasataan when landing in abaddon and realizing Ethereal hadn't brought Gloria with her.

Lucifer, seeing them naked, entwined in each other, became more than the hasataan he had been since the fall. Exploding in rage, he grew a hundred times larger than the first hasataan, made entirely of fire on all parts, a massive trident in his right hand, and in his left he held a new serpent. It was beyond comprehension in size, and it had a face that was not a snake. It was the face of the Angel, Lucifer. All done in silence, when fully grown, he let out a roar of rage as he rose directly above them, laying face down over them, and his left hand let go of the serpent to take them both.

The Vision stopped. It was frozen on the image of Lucifer's face as he, as serpent, was about to devour them. All faces were frozen, stunned, wordless. Gloria stood in front of the Vision as it stayed showing the sick face.

"Well, I have to admit it was even more of a surprise than when I cried out 'dad!' when I saw you two going at it under the apple tree. He was one upset dude, that's for sure. So, what could two young lovers do?"

Stepping away, the Vision continued as the serpent swooped down to them. In the same instant, Gloria's Blade was in her hands, her crystal armor covering her. The new Angel was clad in massive armor and two giant bolts of power were in his hands. At the speed of thought they attacked the monster. The lightening bolts instantly cut the serpent from hasataan's body, then began slicing its body to shreds of red mist, the whole form turning to vapor from the rage shown by the new Angel to protect Gloria. Turning to her and the head of the serpent, though no longer a part of the body, it was fully alive and powerful, and it looked at Gloria, it's forked tongue nearing her as she stood without moving. It stopped in front of her, and she stood with her Blade down at her side, looking into his eyes. It seemed as if time froze. It was Lucifer and Gloria, head to head, the final battle, the time each had waited all eternity for.

All waited for the Blade to strike, but Gloria stood still, and Lucifer did not move. They looked at each other. The battle was over. What Lucifer had sought his entire existence was no more. Gloria was a virgin no longer. She would never be his in any way. By force or even love. He had lost his holy war. He had traveled to the end of existence to find what the Father knew was there.

Nothing.

Then a scene that would be spoken of for all existence to come. Gloria remained standing as if a statue as the serpent transformed to the form of Lucifer when he was a First Angel. He stood before her, crying, yet refusing to say he was sorry. Instead, he walked to her, stood in front of her, then knelt down and told her it was time for suffering to end.

Gloria did something not even the Father could have imagined.

By T. Ulick   217

She handed Lucifer the handle of her Blade.

Looking up to her and nodding, he raised it in front of himself, upwards, and with one swipe with great might struck himself from the top of his head, down his body, and he was no more. The Blade flew back to her hand, and she put it behind her head under her hair. The new Angel had been floating above ready to strike if Lucifer had made any move to harm her, and she raised her hand to him to join her at her side.

The final scene of the Vision was both of them ascending into the nothingness beyond nothing, their armor fading, their bodies naked once more, and they made love in a place where none had gone before.

As the Vision faded, Father, Michael and Elsa turned to look at them and express their shock, but they were gone. Looking up, Elsa said they had left for their home, and she hope to visit them one day when Michael was ready to read the revised edition of her book, *Secrets of the Infinite Scroll.*

About the Author

Author, publisher, photographer and designer, Terry Ulick created the *T: Demonic Investigator Series*, and *Folk Ballads Realized* series of novels for Wherever Books.

Publisher of underground newspapers, consumer magazines, books and a glamour photographer, Terry has a career spanning 50 years of creative works including self-help and empowerment books. When covering rock music in the late 60s and early 70s he interviewed famous rock artists, learning their music was often influenced by folk ballads hundreds of years old. That inspired the *Folk Ballads Realized* series. His life experiences shaped his books about Angels and demons.

"In my books I take all my life events, which are not typical of most people, and reflect on how I've come face-to-face with evil many times. How many people can hitchhike, get picked up by John Wayne Gacy and live to tell the tale? That was meeting a true demon. Evil exists. I had a near-death experience that was beyond imagination. I have experienced the Divine... and a very beautiful Angel who can't be described in human concepts. In my latest book, Wrath of the Angel, *I wished to show how we are capable of love, understanding, and kindness... and smart enough to not fall for evil disguised as attraction. We all have free will. We all need to use it and walk away from evil."*

By T. Ulick

ALSO AVAILABLE FROM WHEREVER BOOKS:

T: Demonic Investigator Series:
Voice in the Night
Demons, Angels & Battle
Death Do Us Part
Angels & Demons Unleashed
Ecstasy of Surrender
The Blessing of Redemption
Six Satans

Also Available:
Folk Ballads Realized Series
The Faire
Fair and Tender Maidens
Wild Mountain Thyme
3 Ravens

View and Purchase at:

www.whereverbooks.com

ROKU Channels:

Angels on Earth
Demonic Investigator
Wherever Books

CPSIA information can be obtained
at www.ICGtesting.com
Printed in the USA
LVHW040423141123
764100LV00042B/45

9 798988 049043